BLIND CHARLIE'S CORNER

by

TIMOTHY P. BANSE

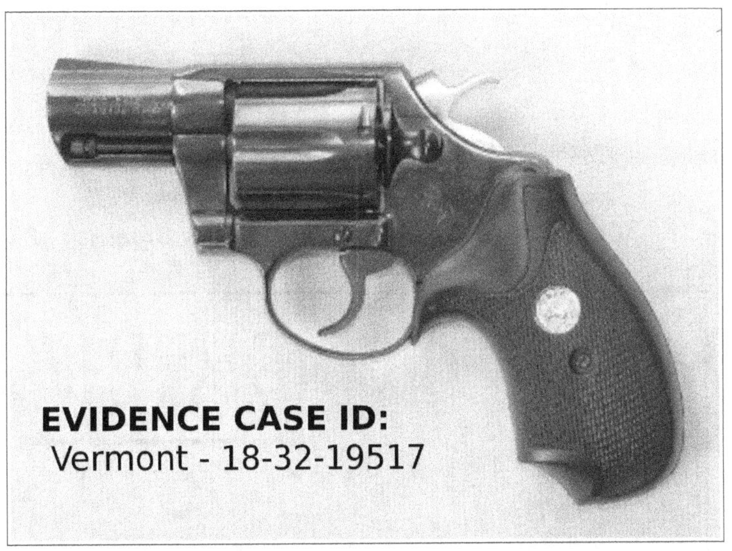

Blind Charlie's Corner
By Timothy P. Banse
© Copyright 2019 - All Rights Reserved
Editor@Middle-Coast-Publishing.com
ISBN-13: 978-0-934523-85-1

Publisher's Cataloging-in-Publication Data

Names: Banse, Timothy P., author.
Title: Blind Charlie's corner / by Timothy P. Banse.
Description: Iowa City, IA: Middle Coast Publishing, 2019.
Identifiers: ISBN 978-0-934523-85-1
Subjects: LCSH Survival--Fiction. | Airplane crash survival--Fiction. | Air travel--Fiction. | Musicians--Fiction. | Rock music--Fiction. | Detective and mystery stories. | BISAC FICTION / General
Classification: LCC PS3602.A668 B53 2019 | DDC 813.6—dc23

"Good Books Are Where We Find Our Dreams . . ."

Iowa City, Iowa

Lyrics to Blind Charlie's hit song:

Flying Blind

Flying blind.
To the place where all the walls are dirty.
A scat talk musician,
tastes the first night's set,
with blood on the needle.
In a scum brown world,
shooting cottons begins.
The scat talk musician,
hoping to turn the flip side of fame.
Flying blind.
Trying to turn off fate
Trying not to fry his mind.
In a scum brown world,
Flying blind.

Chapter One

There is no doubt Dangerous Dave knew better than to do what he was about to do.

The wicked Nor'easter had already dumped a foot of wet snow on the slopes near Burlington, Vermont. So naturally, it followed all the New England ski lodge owners were rubbing their hands together in glee in anticipation of all the pending business. Cold, white gold.

But while the blanket of heavy snow was welcome news for Stowe's downhill skiers, the winter storm was not good news for the veteran pilot, Dangerous Dave Pieczysnki. Visibility was severely limited at the podunk FBO, where his plane sat on the tarmac being fueled. The ceiling was low, less than 500 feet. On the other hand, the instrument-rated pilot had logged many thousands of hours in the seat of his de Havilland Beaver, a lot of that time as a bush pilot out of Fairbanks, Alaska, flying in inclement Arctic weather. So far, he had only crash-landed twice.

The one nagging complication with the wicked weather was that the rock group he had been hired by to ferry around New England from gig to gig positively had to be in Boston later that night for its sold-out concert.

"Gotta be there," Blind Charlie, the leader of the band, told Dave. "Got to," he demanded.

Performing due diligence, the pilot dutifully phoned the Federal Aviation Administration to gain insight into the situation. The news on the weather was not good.

"Are you nuts?" said the FAA guy in the tower. "Nobody in their right mind flies in this weather. You, of all people, know what could happen."

Yes, Dangerous Dave knew all about old pilots and bold pilots. He had sorrowfully attended more than one closed casket funeral service for a fellow aviator who had suffered a fatal case of what pilots not so affectionately refer to as: "Got-to-get-there-itis."

"No go," repeated Dangerous Dave, shaking his head stubbornly.

"But our gig, man," implored Blind Charlie. "Boston."

Dave shook his head no for a third time, pointing to the overcast sky dumping snow on the tarmac like there was no tomorrow. "We fly. We die. No go."

Blind Charlie's voice took on a somber tone. "You fly, you sumbitch, or I sue you for every dime you have, including that clunker of an airplane."

Blind Charlie threatened and cajoled, lawsuits, Yelp reviews, any threat he could think of.

Finally, Dave relented. "Get in," he said, jerking his thumb in the direction of the plane, hoping he wouldn't come to regret his decision.

By the time the musicians stowed drums, guitars, and other gear on the plane, it was dark.

The band was none other than the nearly famous Blind Charlie's Corner. They were destined for fame! That message was trumpeted in newspapers and fan magazines around the world. Rolling Stone loved them, often said good things about them, parroting word for word exactly what the promoter had paid them to say.

Dangerous Dave dutifully went through the startup procedure just as he had done a thousand times before.

Pre-flight checklist completed, poised on the apron of the runway, Dave planted both feet hard on the rudder pedals, which did double duty as brakes, locking the plane in position. An ear cocked to the roar of the engine. He advanced the controls of the big, nine-cylinder Pratt & Whitney Wasp Jr. Radial to wide-open-throttle. The plane strained, trying to move forward. It did not budge. Satisfied the 450-horsepower engine was running like a well-oiled machine, he dropped rpm to idle and radioed the tower for takeoff clearance.

"You nuts? This weather?" crackled the astonished reply. "We talked about this."

"Yep. I'm going." Dave made a sideways glance at Blind Charlie strapped into the adjacent seat. Once again, he advanced the big radial to wide-open-throttle. Brakes off this time, the plane began to roll down the runway, slowly at first but inexorably picking up ground speed.

"Your flight plan, you never filed a flight plan!" complained the guy in the tower.

"No time to waste. I am going."

"Yeah, but with this weather, you know full well . . ."

Interrupting, Dave said, "I'm instrument rated. I trust my instruments." Dave turned off the radio, cutting off any further contact with the tower.

"We'll be flying blind," said Charlie, grinning.

Dave ignored the comment, not realizing the reference to Charlie's hit song.

As the wheels crossed the expansion joints in the concrete runway, they tick-tick, tick-ticked. Picking up speed, the tick-ticking came faster and faster, stopping altogether as the Beaver lifted off the ground and lumbered into the night sky.

The Beaver labored to gain altitude: 1,000 feet above ground level, 2000 feet, and climbing, only barely. Textbook rate of climb for the de Havilland Beaver was about 1,000 feet per minute. But on this climb out, in foul weather, they were barely managing 300 feet per minute, as dreadfully slow as an old Douglas C-47 troop plane.

Once at altitude, the plane struggled to stay in the air. Keeping the wings straight and level was a struggle.

About ten minutes into the flight, the aftermarket stall alarm started screaming bloody murder, alerting the pilot that the plane was no longer flying, that it was falling from the sky. No need for the stall alarm. Dave already knew they were in trouble from the frightening loss of altitude he could feel in the seat of his pants and see with his own eyes rapidly spinning towards zero on the altimeter.

"Happy now, you stupid sumbitch," said Dave angrily to Blind Charlie.

"Do something, man," cried out a terrified, Blind Charlie.

Having fallen to nearly ground level, Dave switched on the landing light and shouted, "Going to try to crash land."

Illuminated in the brilliant loom of a couple of million candlepower landing lights, Dave was startled to see a stand of tall pine trees with a big, wooden barn right behind it, smack dab in his flight path. "Bad news," he muttered to himself.

From flight training, he knew exactly what to do. Long ago, his flight instructor had rather sagely advised, "In a forced landing, if you don't like what you see when you turn on the landing light, turn it back off."

Without a word, Dangerous did. "We are screwed, utterly and completely," he muttered, closing his eyes, bracing for the world of hurt he knew was coming.

Dangerous Dave had disobeyed the laws of physics, and for his mortal sin, he was about to be severely punished.

A moment later, the Beaver made brutal contact with a series of immovable objects. Tree limbs ripped off the rear stabilizer and left it hanging in the branches like an oversize Christmas tree ornament. With an earth-shattering smash, the plane slammed into the side of the barn. Boards and beams splintered and flew through the air like there had been an explosion. Both wings sheared off at their roots, like a kid pulling the wings off a bug. Both wingtip fuel tanks ruptured and spilled many gallons of AvGas. Disemboweled by barn boards, the belly tank split open, spilling more fuel.

When the broken airplane came to rest in the haymow, it was dead.

Chapter Two

Awicked Nor'easter was dumping a mountain of wet snow across the length and breadth of New England.

Detective Kurt Donner was suffering from cabin fever, SAD, or Seasonal Affective Disorder, as the police psychiatrist called it. He was, as they say, climbing the walls with boredom.

Donner owned a Fire Cracker Red, 4-Wheel Drive Jeep Wrangler. Unlike mere All Wheel Drive Jeeps, his boasted true all-weather capability. Bad roads, snow, and ice were never a problem. So he decided to go out for a beer. One and only one beer.

The Buttercup was a rundown, towny bar that reeked of stale beer and loneliness. Its worn-out bar stools leaked stuffing onto the floor, where the fabric mixed with cigarette butts and tracked-in dirt. The edges of the bar top were worn smooth from decades worth of drunks with liquor-softened gums rubbing anxious elbows while guarding a mug of beer like an inmate zealously guarded his tray of food in the joint.

So far as he knew, not a soul in the Buttercup knew Donner or what he did for a living. He found comfort in that anonymity. It was one of his cardinal rules in life to never spend time in any establishment where anyone knew him to be a cop.

His reasoning was as sound as the sea is salt. In holdups, if one of the patrons knew you were a cop, they'd stare right at you, figuring since you were a Law Enforcement Officer, you would do something about the situation. Right?

No big surprise, down through the years, more than

one off-duty cop had been gunned down by a methed-out kid with a shotgun because a cop's friend in the bar blew his cover.

For the same reason, whenever detective Donner sat down for pie and coffee in any cafe, he did not do what all of his other brothers in blue did.

Typically in restaurants and bars off duty cops sit in the far corner facing the door, with their back to the wall to better monitor everything going on. No surprises was the strategy.

The only problem with that scenario, seasoned, armed robbers know to look for the guy in the back booth, figuring him to be a cop. Right or wrong, a guy in the corner would be the first one shot. A preemptive strike. Just in case.

For these reasons, Donner carried himself as a gray man. Nondescript dress, no actions or words to draw attention to him. He did not stand out. He blended in. Five minutes after he left a joint, no one would remember he had ever been there.

On that particular, snowy night, Donner sat quietly at the Buttercup, sipping a bottle of Harp beer and thinking about nothing in particular other than how good it felt to get out of his house.

A bunch of guys stood around the pool table guzzling beer like there was no tomorrow and talking loudly about basketball. There was so much snow coming down the satellite TV was out. So the screen was blank.

Some in the crowd were bikers, the BMW variety, not Harley-Davidson. Some were factory workers from the Thom McCann shoe factory down the road who had stopped off for a beer after their shift before finally going home to the wife and kids.

But there was this one guy garbed in an army fatigue shirt and blue jeans, wearing a green beret and strutting around like a great god of war. Trouble in the making predicted Donner.

Donner pegged the guy as a wannabe, someone who had never done anything more dangerous in actual life than playing the Call to Duty video game. Behind him, he could hear the wannabe getting louder and louder by the minute, bragging about his glory days in the army. The sole survivor of his platoon or some such nonsense. All those dead buddies left behind. Feel pity for me. At the same time, fear me. That was his life script. Vietnam, Iraq, Panama, Afghanistan: Whichever war he claimed to have fought in didn't matter. No one was listening to his senseless babblings.

Donner sighed, thinking it was time for him to depart the premises before the drunk got too excited and incited a ruckus. Donner wanting no drama in his life, picked up his change from the bar top and began to stuff the bills in his wallet. He decided to leave a dollar tip for the bartender.

The murmuring in the background went silent.

Someone in the crowd gasped.

"Put that thing away, Duncan," commanded the bartender from behind the bar. "Now."

"Oh, hell," muttered Donner. Too late, he mused. Draining the last of his beer, he wished he had left a minute sooner.

Out of the corner of his eye, Donner saw that the loud-mouthed drunk, garbed in an OD fatigue shirt and green beret, was now brandishing a Colt 1911 semi-auto handgun.

Donner sighed again and slowly got up off his bar stool. Like it or not, it looked like he would have to get involved.

Donner sized up the situation in an instant. He didn't figure the drunk was likely to shoot up the bar, even as intoxicated as he appeared to be. The only salient danger would be if one of the tough guys at the pool table tried to take the gun away from him. If that happened, innocent people could get hurt.

Or if a cop driving by looked in the window and saw a man waving a gun, that would likely end in the drunk getting shot.

Slowly and deliberately, Donner ambled over towards the drunk.

The drunk stared blankly at him. Hand shaking, his finger curled inside the trigger guard, the Colt bobbled up and down in the wannabe's grip. At least the hammer wasn't cocked. It would have to be thumbed back before it could be fired.

Donner pointed to the pistol, "Wow. Colt Commander. How cool is that."

By then, the two men stood toe to toe. The drunk's eyes were glassy and bloodshot. His breath smelled like a proverbial brewery.

Donner pointed to the Colt, "Never seen one in real life before. Just pictures in gun magazines and on Google."

The drunk's expression softened. Smiling pridefully, he said. "Caliber 45. ACP. A real man stopper."

"Yep, yep, a military round. She's real pretty," said Donner. "Can I look at it?"

Duncan's face transformed from a wannabe warmonger to that of a father who had just been told his infant son was as handsome as blazes. Proudly, he presented his pride and joy, the Colt, to Donner.

Donner reverently held the weapon in both hands, admiring it. "Cool!" he repeated. "So cool." Calmly, he pressed the release, dropped the magazine with 7-rounds fully loaded into his free hand, and shoved it into his pant's pocket. Next, he racked the slide, ejecting a live round from the chamber. Catching the cartridge in midair, he slipped the round into his pocket along with the magazine.

Donner wasn't done.

As fast as lightning, he field stripped the Colt, removing the slide replete with barrel and sticking those parts in his pant's pocket as well.

"Hey!" stammered Duncan. "You can't do that!"

Donner grinned, holding the bare frame in his hand. "Just did, friend."

Pants starting to sag from the weight of the pistol parts, Donner secured the Colt frame in his armpit long enough to hitch up his trousers and tighten his belt a notch.

Looking confused, the drunk's mouth moved, but no words came out.

The bystanders were breathlessly watching the show, a few with open mouths. The bartender could have sold bags of popcorn to go along with the show.

"Besides." With his free hand, Donner reached into his back pants pocket, pulled out his badge, and swept it in a wide arc, first showing it to Duncan and then to the bikers and factory workers gathered around the pool table.

"I want it back. My gun. I want it back," pouted Duncan. "Paid pert-near nine hunnerd dollars for it."

"Shuddup, Duncan," said one woman.

"You want to go to jail tonite?" said Donner, in a calming voice. Staring straight into Duncan's eyes, he was looking deep into the man's soul, trying to read how his ego was reacting to having just had his pistol taken away, by guile, of all things.

Donner repeated the question, "You want to go to jail tonite?" A textbook technique, the threat of jail often calmed civilians enough to end a volatile situation.

"Nnno," stammered Duncan.

"Then shut up. Call a cab. Go home."

"Already called one," said the bartender. "Uber. Five

minutes out."

Donner pointed to the door and stared hard at Duncan.

Duncan hesitated.

"Go home, Duncan," said Donner. "Or go to jail."

Duncan slunk out the door like a dog with his tail between his legs. A rush of cold, outside air sent a shiver up Donner's spine.

"Buy you a drink," offered the bartender.

"No thanks," Donner observed his self-imposed limit. Rule of One, he called it. Just one beer or whiskey when driving. One and only one, then it was time to go home.

When Donner saw Duncan get in the Uber, he headed outside to his Jeep, begrudging the fact that he had burned yet another place to hang out in. But at the same time, he was consoled by the fact that he had just added another eminently collectible firearm to his collection.

Standing in the fresh night air on the sidewalk outside the Buttercup, his breath frosting, he clapped his gloved hands together a couple of times to warm them. The snow was coming down, he mused. Looking up and down the street, he smiled. Blanketed in fresh white snow, his little burg, his Shiretown, looked breathtakingly beautiful, like a Currier and Ives print of small-town New England from another time.

Donner decided he wasn't quite ready to go home yet. He was as hungry as a starving wolf.

Chapter Three

onner had no worries about his blood alcohol level with a single beer under his belt. So he drove six blocks down the highway to Rosie's Diner, a greasy spoon at the edge of Shiretown, on the north edge of city limits just before the single-family homes gave way to forest and rolling hills.

What made this Rosie's place special was its status as a stainless steel diner, a genuine Mahoney, built in 1938. A converted Pullman railroad car, replete with stainless steel siding, a pink, green and yellow, neon sign blinked:

Open 24 hours

For the most part, Yelp reviews said mostly good things about Rosie's Diner. Reading the litany of comments, you could tell which ones had been salted like gold nuggets in a played-out mine and which ones were written by patrons who had actually dined there. Comfort food said one satisfied customer. Yum, said another. Not clean, said yet another.

The narrow dining area featured a long, sit-down counter with stools running the length of the car and a row of booths running parallel. The interior was tablecrafted with red and white checkered table cloths and plain white china. The owners had adorned the ceiling with a million vintage hubcaps (Rambler, Willys, Ford, Edsel, Packard, Chevy, Plymouth) collected over the decades. Donner caught an aromatic whiff of roast beef and carrots.

True to the critical Yelp review, Rosie's place was filthy. The front windows needed cleaning, the floors needed mopping badly. The men's restroom was out of order: A hand-lettered sign directed men to knock first, then use the Ladies. And be sure to lift the lid, please.

Most of the seats at the tables were occupied by the dinner crowd finishing dessert and coffee. In sharp contrast, most of the counter stools sat empty. Donner took one at the counter, right upfront, close to the door.

The clean-scrubbed waitress, a pretty brunette in her 20s, smelled of lovely perfume. Her name tag declared, Tilly! Not just plain, old, Tilly, but Tilly! Replete with an exclamation mark!

Donner figured the exclamation mark was Tilly's way of proclaiming that she was special. You know, a narcissist. He sighed. At least the woman didn't have a tattoo. At least, not one he could see with all of her clothes on.

Tilly smiled, putting a white mug of coffee down on the counter in front of him, along with a bundle of flatware rolled up tightly in a white napkin. She handed him a menu, then pertly bounced off down the counter with her carafe of coffee, sloshing in time to each step, stopping at each table to top off mugs. Tilly worked for tips and took her work very seriously.

Perusing the menu, Donner instantly focused on the dinner specials: Venison stew, the first item at the top. The price was right, about what he would have paid for a fast-food cheeseburger and Pepsi. So when Tilly came back with pen and pad in hand to take his order, he told her he would have venison stew.

She shook her head." Unh-uh. No. All gone. None left. Sorry. No can do."

"Sounds like you have a hundred ways to say no." Donner had encountered the same scenario in dozens of podunk diners. If you were a local known to the establishment, you were served venison, bear, pheasant breast on wild rice, or any other wild game entrées that appeared on the menu seasonally. But if you were a stranger in town, it was a different story, "Sorry. We just ran out."

This was just one of the contraindications of his incognito strategy. He was a local but a stranger in Rosie's Diner.

Donner knew from personal experience the "Sorry. We just run out" excuse was nothing more than a ploy intended to soothe the hurt feelings of a rejected diner who could see wild game entrées on folk's dinner plates on tables all around him. The same entrées he had just been denied.

Donner knew this duplicity was no more complicated than the management did not want to share the good stuff with outsiders, wanting instead to take care of regular customers. The restaurateurs' bread and butter, so to speak.

Donner stared hard at Tilly.

She stared back just as hard.

"So, where did the venison come from?" said Donner.

She stammered, "Game warden? Doe got hit out on Fire Lane Road by a pickup truck. He put it out of its misery and give it to Rosie. Sorry, we're out. Is meatloaf okay? Home-cooked."

Tilly had lied to him through her as-bright-as-the-driven-snow-white-teeth, teeth gleaming, so brilliantly that it was apparent, she had chemically whitened them. Tilly crossed her arms, holding the order pad tightly against her heart.

Donner knew Tilly was lying about the venison.

She knew he knew she was lying.

Still staring, all the while smiling like an angel from heaven, Donner politely said, "Do me a favor. Tilly. Why don't you check with the manager? See if there's not maybe just one more portion left in the stew pot. With lots more meat than carrots and spuds."

His smile dissolved. "Did I forget to mention I tip? I am a big tipper. Thirty percent. Always. Thirty percent. Cash."

She blinked, rolled her eyes, and stomped towards the back, returning a few moments later with a generous bowl of stew, overflowing with succulent chunks of venison swimming in thick, brown gravy with a sprinkling of carrots and potatoes.

"Your lucky day," she said, setting it on the counter in front of him. "Found some. Had to scrape the bottom of the barrel. Now we are out. For certain," she nodded. Her head bobbed up and down like a wobbly head on a car's dashboard.

Donner mirrored her body language, nodding back in appreciation. "Thanks," he said.

She sauntered off, in her mind adding his promised big tip to her daily score.

Donner took a big spoonful. Chewing the succulent meat, savoring the flavour, he remembered why he liked wild game so much. It had flavor, unlike factory farm meat bought at the grocery. Wild game flavor was as distinct from farm-raised beef as was the difference between free-range scrambled eggs from hens that pecked at the dirt and ate Marigolds and the eggs from hens confined to cages with a thousand other sickly, factory chickens.

Tilly was back a minute later with a bottle of Narragansett and a frosty beer glass. Condensation dripped down the sides of the chilled, green bottle. "Pairs well with venison stew," she said, up-selling.

He waved her off. "Tempting, but no thanks," he said, observing his self-imposed rule of just one beer or whiskey when driving. One and only one.

Behind him, the door swung open, letting in a draft of frigid air. A couple of rough-looking construction workers shuffled in, stomping their boots and tracking clods of brown dirt onto the already dirty floor. They were dressed like twins, garbed in matching Woolrich flannel lumberjack shirts and matching, brown Carhartt canvas jeans, cinched with thick brown leather belts. Facts be known, the two men were identical twins, the Smith brother twins.

"Hi ya', boys," said Tilly.

As the two men took a stool at the counter next to Donner, the taller one answered, "Eve-nin, sparkles. How's yer ma?"

"Better now, thank you. Medication's finally working. Feeling well enough, she come in and baked some Georgia peach pies this morning."

"Glad to hear it," said Binnie, the older of the two Smith twins. "Rosie's a good woman. Miss her at church on Sundays. Choir's not the same without her," he grumped.

"What can I getcha, Binnie? Hope you're hungry."

"I am surely hungry. Me and Hendry been out at the job site excavating footings all day long. Damn wind. Stomachs been growling for hours. Hear ya' got some venison stew tonight. How about a bowl of that along with some of your ma's peach pie."

Tilly wrote Binnie's order down on the green pad. "And what about you, Hendry, want some stew? Cheeseburger?"

Hendry studied the menu for a second, running his finger down the list of specials, then said, "Naw, I'll have venison steak. And a side of fried potatoes with onions, I guess."

"We got venison liver today," she offered.

Hendry squinted his eyes, studying the menu. "Don't

see it."

"Not exactly on the menu," she whispered conspiratorially. "But we got it."

"Hot damn," he said, slapping the top of the counter top with the palms of both hands. "Change my order to that. Tell Stinky to make sure the meat is bloody. For Pete's sake, don't overcook it this time."

"You got it," she nodded.

Hendry held up his index finger to make a point, "And I still want my fried potatoes and onions. Lossa onions," he added.

"You got it," she repeated, disappearing through the stainless, bat wing doors into the kitchen.

Liver. Donner sighed. Off-menu items. This was another greasy spoon enigma. If he had known about the venison liver, he would have ordered that instead of venison stew. Now halfway through dinner, he was considering asking Tilly to package his stew in a to-go box and having liver. Ultimately, he decided it would be too much bother. Besides, they might be out of venison liver.

Some men are born in the wrong century.

Donner sighed, wishing he had been born in another time, another place. He just didn't feel as if he fit in with modern society, that had he lived in a different era, he would have enjoyed life more. If he had his druthers, he would have been born a hundred and fifty years earlier and trapped beaver in the Frontier West. Probably would have taken a pretty Indian woman for a wife, he reckoned.

Growing up, one of his boyhood idols had been the infamous mountain man, Liver-Eating Johnson, alternatively known as Crow Killer Johnson. That would be the Crow Indian tribe, not the black-feathered crow related to the raven and jackdaw.

Johnson, a trapper in the American West during the

early 1800s, was renowned for shooting deer with his .50 caliber flintlock Hawken rifle, opening up the abdominal cavity, slicing off a slab of bloody, liver and consuming it raw. Blood dribbling down his chin and all. Some historians claim he did the same thing to Crow Indians he had killed in battle.

It helps to understand Johnson's savagery by learning that eating raw liver from freshly-killed deer, as well as the livers of both Indians and White men killed in battle, was a grisly, frontier tradition, much like the taking of scalps. Donner's college American History professor had once dourly said in class, "You can't judge the past from today's standards of decency."

The thought occurred to Donner that maybe he ought to do what Liver-Eating Johnson had done a hundred fifty years before: Go deer hunting with a muzzle-loading Hawken just like Johnson had carried. Only Donner's black powder rifle would be cap and ball instead of a flintlock. In his mind's eye, he could see himself hunkered down at a flickering campfire feasting on raw, bloody deer liver.

Still wouldn't be the same, he mused. Modern-day hunters don't hunt. They don't stalk. They ambush. Perched high up in a tree stand, sipping copious amounts of Brandy in their coffee, they lie in wait for the sun to come up, then shoot an unsuspecting buck as it walks past on the forest floor below. No sport in that. None.

Sitting at Rosie's lunch counter, bathed in the green glow of fluorescent lighting, Donner began to notice the construction workers' overpowering body odor. More precisely, they stank to high heaven. Out of the corner of his eye, he surreptitiously looked them over. Both men were filthy dirty: Clothes torn and crudely patched; Leather scuffed off the toes of their safety boots, exposing the steel plates to the elements, freckled with rust. The

Smith brothers would qualify for Grunge Quarterly magazine, he mused.

Hendry, sitting next to him, had a particularly filthy face. Particles of dirt embedded in the pores of his skin lent his complexion a black, speckled appearance. Most of his fingernails were either broken or tinged purple and black. The skin on his fingers and the palms of his hand looked heavily calloused. This was a man who worked with his hands for his daily bread. For his venison liver.

Ignoring the potent smell, Donner was glad he was already more than halfway through his meal. He took another bite of stew.

In mere minutes, Tilly had put two meals on the counter in front of the boys, saying in a cheery voice, "Here ya' go, boys." That's the thing about daily specials. They are prepared and ready and waiting back in the kitchen for shorter ticket times and happier customers. She popped the caps on two bottles of Narragansett. No glasses. The boys always drank their beer straight from the bottle.

Binnie took a long pull, "Ah, that's so good."

Hendry just guzzled beer and shoveled food into his mouth.

Donner lightly nudged Hendry in the ribs to get his attention.

He paused, a forkful of liver halfway to his mouth. "What?" he grumped.

"Who's Stinky?" asked Donner.

"Cook," said Hendry. "Ya' shoulda been able to figure that out by yourself, feller with your good looks and high IQ."

Donner went on. "So where'd he get the nickname, Stinky?"

Talking with his mouth full of liver, Hendry said, "Fits 'em. Cuz he stinks worse than a graveyard outhouse."

Binnie jabbed his fork in the general direction of the kitchen, "That's why Rosie makes him stay in the back. So he don't offend customers none."

Out of Hendry's view, Tilly arched her eyebrows, grimaced, then hooked her thumb in the brother's direction, mouthing, "PU."

Donner chuckled, pointed at Hendry's venison liver and onions, and mumbled, "Bon Appetite, my friend."

Hendry saluted him back with his long neck Narragansett.

Donner took another hearty spoonful of stew. "Good. Very meaty," he said to no one in particular. A few bites later, done eating, he pushed the bowl away.

On cue, Tilly appeared. "How'd the food taste? Good?"

He wiped his mouth clean with a napkin. "Yeah, good, fine."

"Anything else?" She asked pen in hand, poised to total the bill.

"Yep. Peach pie. Any good?"

"Georgia Peach Pie, she corrected, then leaned forward to whisper, "Let you in on a secret. Ma bakes it. Born and raised on a little farm outside of Valdosta. Better than good," she giggled. "Wicked good!" The girl had a nice smile when she didn't blind you with the light reflecting off her chemically-whitened teeth.

Moments later, she was back with a slice of Georgia Peach pie topped with a dollop of whipped cream. Setting it down on the counter, she waggled a finger, warning, "Mind ya, don't complain about the gap between the top crust and the fillin'." Happens when pie's baked at high heat. Crust sets before the peach filling cooks down some."

Donner dug his fork into the pie's golden-brown crust and took a bite. She was right. It was wicked good. Just like the stew had been wicked good. The Yelp reviewers had been faithful to their word. For the most part.

From the flaky crust, Donner could tell her ma baked with honest to goodness lard in the recipe instead of the hydrogenated glop most modern-day cooks use. Like a starving wolf, he ate every last crumb and licked a finger full of the sweet peach filling off the plate.

Tilly, smiling, was back with the bill.

Donner studied it, doing the math in his head cynically musing how waiters were also so much more pleasant at the end of the meal when you were considering how big of a tip to leave.

Ultimately, he laid out ten dollars for venison stew, Georgia Peach pie, and the bottomless cup of coffee. He calculated how much a 30 percent of that would be. Feeling generous, he laid a five-dollar bill on top of the ten.

Wide-eyed in disbelief, Hendry stared at the money. He nudged his brother Binnie and pointed to the ten and the five-dollar bills laid down on the counter by Donner's pie plate.

"What ya doing?" asked Binnie, incredulously. He pointed with his fork at the money. "Not leaving a five-dollar bill for a tip, are you?"

Donner was taken aback. "Well, how much should I leave then? A dollar?"

"My Lord, no," murmured Binnie, shaking his head in disbelief.

Hendry put down his beer bottle and added his two cents worth. "A dime. Leave the girl a dime."

Binnie chimed in once again, enunciating each word one at a time, "One-thin-dime. Don't ya get it? Her momma owns this restaurant. I know you heard her say it. She brags on it to everybody."

Hendry pointed to the neon sign outside blinking: Rosie's - Rosie's - Rosie's. "She don't need that kind of money." He shook his head in disbelief.

Hendry nudged Binnie, then jerked a thumb in Donner's direction. "Must be an outta stater. Leaf peeper."

"City slicker, "added Binnie. Prolly drives a bright and shiny orange Volvo with a Save the Whales bumper sticker." The twins turned around to look out the window into the parking lot to confirm, but it was too dark to identify what kind of car he drove.

"Bon appétit," scoffed Hendry, further mocking Donner.

Another customer walked in through the door, bringing a gust of frigid air in with him. He stood patiently waiting at the cash register. In sharp contrast to the Filthy Brothers, the newcomer was clean-shaven, hair neatly combed. His powder blue Columbia down-jacket looked brand new. Neatly pressed blue jeans showed razor-sharp creases down the front of the pant legs.

Tilly approached with a big smile. "To-go order for you and Nancy?"

"Yes," said the man, smiling. "What's on special?"

"Venison stew, venison steak, venison liver. Oh, and meatloaf. Not venison. Normal."

Tilly looked over to Donner.

Their eyes locked.

"Venison," mouthed Donner.

Her face reddened. She looked away. "Thought we were out earlier, but there's plenty left."

The newcomer made up his mind in a Boston instant. "Make it venison stew. Two bowls. "He held up two fingers.

Looking over to see what the Smith brothers were eating for dessert, Maynard pantomimed, tipping his hat, "Brothers Smith. Evening."

Binnie said, "Hiya, Maynard."

Hendry grunted his hello.

"How's the peach pie tonite?" he asked.

"Georgia Peach pie," said Tilly softly.

The brothers grunted in unison. "Good. Wicked good."

"Two slices, then," Maynard told Tilly. "Along with venison stew. Did I mention it's to go? I'd surely order pie a la mode, but even in this weather, afraid it would melt. Might not be able to eat right away if she's busy again."

"Like it always is with you two," Tilly replied good-naturedly. "Give me a minute, Maynard. I got this."

Promptly she returned from the kitchen with a brown paper bag. Giving it to Maynard, she kept her hand steady on the bottom, supporting the weight of the venison stew so the to-go containers wouldn't Kamikaze crash through the bottom of the paper bag and mess the linoleum floor worse than it already was.

"Put in a little container of Bourbon whipped creme for pie topping," she said. "No charge. Won't melt like ice cream if she gets delayed." Tilly rang up the order, took his money, and deposited the bills in the cash drawer. "Say hi to Nancy for me."

"Will do." Maynard stuffed a five in the tip jar next to the register. He turned, smiled at Tilly, then walked out the door, letting in another blast of cold air.

"Nice guy, Maynard," said Tilly, picking up Donner's payment and walking to the cash register to ring it up. "I ever get married. I want a man like him. Devoted to his wife. Brings Nancy dinner every night at the hospital. Isn't that romantic?"

"She sick or something?" said Donner.

"No, silly," said the waitress. "Nancy's an emergency room nurse. Works second shift."

"Hear tell Maynard had a hard time in the war," remarked Binnie.

"'Splains that far-off stare he gets sometimes," added Hendry. "Sometimes he gets wound up tighter than an idiot's watch."

"Him and cousin Edgar," said Binnie.

"War is a racket," said Hendry.

"I won't disagree," said Binnie.

Donner's cellphone vibrated like an angry bee.

A text message alerted him there had been a shooting. He would have to drive a couple of miles to the hospital on the other side of town to interview a perpetrator

who had suffered some sort of mishap during an arrest.

Donner sighed. At least this time, he had finished eating before duty called.

Trudging to his Jeep, he noticed a lot of snow had fallen while he had been inside eating supper. The roads would be slippery, as slick as ice. He was glad his Jeep had 4-Wheel Drive and that he hadn't drunk the second Narragansett. Once again, in his life, his strict Rule of One had paid a big dividend.

Chapter Four

Maynard Reece pulled into the Shiretown Consolidated Hospital emergency room parking lot. He sat there parked, engine idling, heater blowing full blast. Big, wet snowflakes landed on the windshield. Wiper blades swished back and forth, smearing snow into water. He was as warm as toast.

Maynard marked time waiting in his car for the simple reason an ambulance had just sped in ahead of him, lighting up the parking lot and the sides of the building with the eerie red glow of flashing lights.

The lights and blaring siren went dead.

Maynard looked on as a frantic team of EMTs maneuvered a gurney out the back of the ambulance, down onto the pavement, and rolled it hurriedly into the Trauma Center.

He turned up the volume on the radio, figuring to kill time listening to WBZ Boston. Sitting there alone in the dark, listening to the radio while watching the snow come down, it was a beautiful night. Peaceful, he mused.

The brown paper bag sitting on the seat next to him emanated the delicious aroma of venison stew, deceptively smelling like beef and carrots. Maynard sighed. It looked like he wouldn't be eating supper with his wife any time soon. He was glad he hadn't opted for peach pie a la mode. Make that Georgia peach pie, he corrected himself, smiling.

Sitting there warm, comfortable, and in peace, he grew restless. After a few minutes, he grabbed the fragrant bag off the seat and got out of the car. "What the heck," he mused. "Maybe it's nothing serious."

He hoped.

As it turned out, he was wrong.

Walking in through the ER entrance, he could not help but notice a trail of blood running from the back of the ambulance, through the doors, and into trauma, right up to triage: Copious, bright red, blood. So much blood was spilled on the hospital floor he could smell its distinctive coppery taste.

The blood reminded him of another time and place. A dark place in his mind he did not want to revisit. A chill ran up and down his spine. He put it out of his mind. All that blood did not look good for somebody, mused Maynard.

Once inside, the Emergency Room appeared deserted. There was not a soul to be seen. No one sat at the reception desk handing out insurance and admittance forms to fill out. No one sat in the waiting area awaiting news about a friend or loved one. No one killed time mindlessly reading old magazines and sipping bitter coffee.

Like he had done a thousand times before when visiting his wife, Maynard stepped through the double doors and peeked into the treatment area, hoping to catch a glimpse of Nancy. He spotted her busy in one of the bays treating the patient who had just come in by ambulance. Nancy looked radiantly beautiful in her blue scrubs, even though they were splattered crimson. Her face was set in worry lines like she often did when working hard to save a life.

While gazing lovingly at his wife, something startled him. Unseen, someone had come up from behind him, put a hand on his shoulder, and pushed past him, going on into the ER treatment area.

"Pardon," said the someone.

Catching a glimpse as he went by, Maynard recognized

the someone pushing past as a man he had just seen at Rosie's diner, the one who had been sitting by the Smith brothers eating peach pie like a starving wolf.

Maynard wondered what the stranger was doing at the hospital, in the Emergency Room of all places. It was an odd coincidence. He watched someone walk right up to two uniformed cops who were standing in the hallway. He knew both of them: Thorndike and Barnhardt. The two officers and the stranger shook hands then started jabbering.

Maynard casually edged nearer, as close to the trio as he dared, eavesdropping while Thorndike and Barnhardt talked to the guy in plain clothes. Probably a detective surmised Maynard.

Thorndike, a handsome man, resplendent in uniform, looking like some actor from a cop TV show, was reading from his notepad. He started the beginning of his report. "Victim, Earline Yoder. No middle name. Female. Age 26. Caucasian. Pretty girl."

"Perpetrator?" asked Donner.

Thorndike looked up from his notepad and shook his head in disgust. "David Michael House. Age 28. Her estranged husband. Not from around here. A cracker from Charleston. His second marriage. His first wife, a Key West stripper, divorced him when she found out he liked guys too."

"Earline told us she caught him a couple of times too. In flagrante delicto."

Barnhardt, Thorndike's partner, added, "We know the two of them well enough, been to their house a dozen times for domestic abuse calls. Arrested him five times." he shook his head in disgust. "Ain't no fixin' stupid."

Thorndike went on, breathless in the telling of his summation. "Sumbitch shot Earline in both legs at point-blank range with a 12 gauge double barrel, shotgun.

Birdshot did a lot of damage. Nearly severed one of the legs. Lost a lot of blood."

"Where's the shotgun?" asked Donner.

"By now, bagged and in the evidence locker at the station," said Barnhardt.

"Alcohol involved?" asked Donner. If past was prologue, he already knew the answer to that question.

Thorndike said, "Didn't smell any on his breath, probably meth though. Already had the lab draw blood for a toxicology screen."

Barnhardt said, "Damn shame. I knew Earline back in high school. Couple years behind me. Pretty enough, she could have been a Playboy lingerie model. Nice girl. Hurting her is like crushing a flower."

Thorndike nodded in agreement, "Yep. She is gorgeous."

The three cops stared at the long trail of blood on the floor. A custodian was already cleaning it up, but the mop bucket water was diluted and tinged crimson red from blood. All the custodian managed to do was swish red water around the floor tiles. He looked frustrated with his efforts.

Donner mused that the custodian should probably dump the mop bucket, sop up most of the blood with paper towels and start over with fresh water so the mop would clean the floor instead of just swishing around a slurry of blood and water. But Donner kept quiet, not wanting to tell another man how to do his job.

Donner whispered so no one else could overhear. "That kind of damage to her legs, she'll probably never walk again. If she even lives."

Barnhardt fumed. "Get this. He shot Earline after she told him she was getting a divorce, told us if he can't have her, nobody can."

"Got two babies," Thorndike chimed in. "One eight

months, one six years old."

Barnhardt continued. "Get this. Sumbitch shot Earline while she was holding the kids in her arms. She was trying to protect them from him."

Donner raised an eyebrow, fearful of what he was about to hear next.

Thorndike held up a hand to ease Donner's concern. Once again, his voice cracked with the telling. "No. Kids weren't hurt, just scared to death. When we pulled out with him in cuffs, grandma was in the living room trying to get 'em calmed down enough to stop crying so she could take 'em to her place."

From the two young cops' age and emotional reaction, Donner figured both of them to have youngsters of their own at home.

Barnhardt sighed, "For the rest of their lives, poor kids will have to carry the memory of the night daddy shot mommy."

Donner said, "My guess is he won't be getting visitation with the kids, supervised or otherwise, any time soon. He's going to prison for a long time. If she dies, even longer.

Barnhardt said, "I'm glad the death penalty is back. She dies, House goes to the electric chair.

Donner nodded. "By the way, where is he?"

Thorndike jerked a thumb over his shoulder. "Right behind us, behind that white curtain. Bay 2. Handcuffed to the bed. Hope the sumbitch tries to escape. I really do."

Donner furrowed his eyebrows. "Why's he here and not in jail?"

"Requires medical attention," explained Barnhardt.

"Oh. So what happened? He clumsy?" Clumsy was cop code for having been roughed up in custody.

The cop who had shed a tear in telling Earline's story answered. "He fell down. Hard. Bunch of times."

It was clear to Donner precisely who was responsible for the perp's clumsiness. His partner had probably looked the other way when it happened. Over and over again. Or, they had tag teamed.

Donner nodded in understanding. During booking at the jail, he had been there himself, having witnessed scumbag perps, real scum, suddenly become clumsy and fall down a flight of stairs. Sometimes, inexplicably, a scumbag perp fell down the same flight of stairs over and over again in a single night. Clumsy, real clumsy.

The three cops stood in awkward silence until the heart monitor started screaming bloody murder in high-pitched beeps. Earline Yoder's heart had stopped beating. Nurses started shouting the spine-chilling refrain: "Code Blue. Code Blue."

The shock from horrible damage to her legs, loss of blood. The psychological effect of the betrayal by the father of her children had ganged up to overwhelm her heart. It seemed dearly beloved Earline, mother of two, was destined to die. Even if all of the doctors and nurses were able to resuscitate her, there was a question as to what would be revived, an issue of brain damage from lack of oxygen during CPR.

With clenched fists, and red rage burning in his eyes, Thorndike took a step towards the white curtain in front of Bay 2.

He never was able to take a second step.

Both his partner Barnhardt and detective Donner instantly reacted. There was a brief struggle.

"Don't do it, man," said Barnhardt.

"Do you want to go to jail tonite, "said Donner. It was all he could think of to say, feeling as dumb as a road apple the moment it slipped out.

Between the efforts of Donner and his partner, Thorndike calmed down. Regaining his senses, he muttered in frustration, "People are turds." He said it in such a way it looked like he had a mouthful of the stuff.

Donner nodded, "Ain't it the awful truth."

About that time, Donner spotted Maynard, out of the corner of his

eye, still standing by the door. Detective Donner furrowed his brow in concern and turned to face him full-on, "Can I help you?"

Barnhardt said, "He's okay. That's Maynard. His wife is one of the nurses working on Earline. "

"You doing okay tonite, Maynard," asked Thorndike.

Maynard nodded, yes, turned on his heel, and went back out into the waiting room without uttering a single word.

Barnhardt explained. "Maynard's a good guy. Army veteran. Saw a lot of stuff in the war. He's right at home in the ER with all the blood and guts."

Thorndike sagely added, "He'd do to go on patrol with."

"That's some high praise," said Donner, nodding in understanding.

Barnhardt went on, "Like I said, that's his wife in there with the crash cart. Nancy. Nicknamed Nancy Nurse. Call her that because she's such a good nurse."

"Nurse practitioner," corrected officer Thorndike, punctuating his comment with a raised index finger.

"Well," said Donner. "While

Nancy Nurse and everyone else is busy attending to Miss Yoder. Let's the three of us talk to this David Michael House character for a spell. Interrogate him. See if he feels like telling us his side of the story. See if he wants to go for a little walk up and down some stairwells."

Barnhardt and Thorndike looked at each other and grinned in diabolical understanding.

Chapter Five

Blind Charlie had survived the crash, being thrown from the plane, landing hard on a huge heap of a snow bank that only somewhat cushioned the blow. Wind knocked out of him and gasping for breath, he came to consciousness hearing a resounding whump as the plane burst into flames.

The fire accelerated into a bright orange blossom from the ruptured fuel tanks having dumped gasoline into the cabin and overflowing onto bone dry straw and barn boards. Huge clouds of thick, carbon-rich, black smoke billowed up from the wreckage. Within minutes the roof and walls of the barn were engulfed in flames. The plane wreckage, with three dead men inside, burned wildly at the center of the inferno.

Rotting straw on the stable floor, that had been moldering for 20 odd years, began to smolder, then burst into flames releasing the fragrant stench of horse urine and mummified road apples.

From where he lay on the ground, a scant few yards away from the conflagration, Blind Charlie smelled Dangerous Dave and the boys in the band burning to a crisp in the white-hot heat. He thought it ironic how he felt cold from the frozen ground sucking the warmth out of him, yet at the same time the top of his legs and upper body were comfortably warmed from the heat of the funeral pyre.

"Where's Waldo?" he joked. Charlie began to shiver, partly in fear, partly from the intense cold. And partly because their plane had gone down and he had nary a clue where in the world they had crashed: Massachusetts?

Vermont? Mexico?

Shivering, Charlie wished he was wearing his down jacket instead of a vest. Hello," he called out in a plaintiff wail. "Anybody else make it? Guys . . ."

"Over here," came a weak reply. "That you, Charlie? It's me, Mike. Appears we're the only ones alive."

"You hurt?"

Mike Watts answered, "Think I broke my leg. Hurts awful. Can't get up. You?"

"Arm's broke. Be a long time before I play Stairway from Heaven again. From the way it hurts lot of my ribs are broken too."

"Yeah. Me too. Hurts to breathe."

The two rockers lay quietly for a spell listening to the roar of the fire. The stink of wood smoke from the barn boards and the smell of burning bodies made Blind Charlie sick to his stomach. He vomited in the snow.

Watts had to piddle, so he did so, right where he lay. He would come to regret that move in an hour when the fresh puddle of pee he was laying in turned to yellow ice, freezing his designer jeans to the ground.

"Figure Boston show will go on without us?" pondered Charlie, aloud.

Watts chuckled. "Dunno. That's why we have completion insurance. Besides, we got bigger problems."

Once again, the two rockers lay still, listening to the roar of the fire. Every now and then a red, glowing ash would shoot up into the sky only to moments later plummet to the earth like a falling star. Blind as a bat out of hell, Charlie could only hear them sizzle when they hit the snow and were extinguished.

"Where you figure we are?" asked, Charlie. "How long until someone finds us?"

"Figure we came down in the Waxahatchie Wilderness, somewhere this side of Mount Neverclimb."

Truth be told there was no figuring to it. There was no guess and no by golly. Watts knew exactly where they were, having just Googled their exact location on his cellphone. Turning it off to save the battery, he shook his head slowly.

He told Charlie, "Still snowing. Rescue teams won't start looking for us until snow stops. Hours, a day maybe two. We're gonna be here awhile. Especially if snow covers most of the wreckage. From the air all searchers are likely to see is a burned out barn. Not a downed aircraft."

"Your cell phone got bars?"

He lied. "Dunno. Lost it in the crash."

"Well, do you think they'll find us before we freeze to death?"

"We. We won't be making it," Watts said in a somber tone., putting emphasis on the word, we.

Blind Charlie was confused. With his keen hearing he had picked up a not-so-subtle nuance that he did not like in Watt's voice. "What the hell does that mean? We?"

"Simple." Watts paused for a beat before going on. "You're gonna die, Charlie. Right here at the scene of the crash."

Blind Charlie heard Watts rack the action on his Saturday Night Special pistol and say, "Sorry 'bout that."

Blind Charlie recognized the characteristic sound all too well. Like most blind people, Charlie's brain compensated for his loss of hearing by heightening the awareness of his other senses. He could identify people strolling into a room by their distinctive scent and the sound of their footfalls.

"Everybody's gait sounds different," he had once explained to an adoring groupie, making small talk after having just given her the wild ride.

On the street he heard a myriad of sounds most folks

were deaf to. And in everyday conversation he had to really listen to words spoken in order to compensate for missing the clues people gave through their body language. Suffice it to say, his hearing was acute.

With his blindness, Charlie had never actually seen Watts brandishing the handgun, but he had heard other band members talking about it. To hear them tell the story Watts had a little, semi-automatic pistol, a garish, chrome-plated Raven .25 automatic replete with genuine, imitation, ivory grips. Watts had seemed to think the pimp gun impressed small town roadies and groupies. After a gig, in the wee hours of the morning, he had been known to fire off a full magazine of six shots: Pop, pop, pop, pop, pop, pop. Shooting up hotel walls, mirrors, pictures and furniture, his antics left the cloying stink of gunfire in the room. His hotel room antics made Crosby, Stills, Nash and Young look like well-behaved angels.

In his mind's, eye Charlie could see Watts pointing the pistol playfully at him.

"I'm going to shoot you, Charlie," Watts said, his voice as cold as ice.

Charlie heard a sharp, bang and felt intense pain burrow into his left bicep and spread its tentacles to the core of the pain center in his brain. "Ouch," he cried out.

"Ouch," mocked, Watts, laughing like a maniac. "What are you a little girl? Ouch?"

The feint odor of gun smoke drifted over to where Charlie lay bleeding in the snow. He figured out what had just happened.

"Good," said Watts. "You're bleeding like a stuck pig. All part of my plan."

Blind Charlie heard another gunshot and felt intense pain as a bullet struck him for a second time. Only this time his right bicep ached miserably.

Watts cackled, "More blood! Bleed brother, bleed!

You're going to bleed out right here under these trees!"

"But why?" gasped Charlie. "What I ever do to you?"

"You just don't get it, do you? Fate has blessed me with a splendid opportunity. Remember Buddy Holly, Ritchie Valens, Jim Croce, Otis Redding, Patsy Cline, Lynyrd Skynyrd and Ricky Nelson, oh, and John Denver and Jenni Rivera. Remember how all of them died in plane crashes?"

Watts didn't bother waiting for an answer but instead continued his manic rant, "Instantly their music went to the top of the charts making millions. With our plane crash Blind Charlie's Corner stands poised to become world famous and with just me as the lone survivor I won't have to share any loot with you guys. I figure our music rights are worth millions!"

Charlie's' voice was stern. "Not hardly. Stephan Tyler was talking about that recently. Read his interview in Stone. He was whining that a few years ago their music portfolio was worth millions. Not anymore Nobody buys CDs. Ever hear of Spotify? The only money is in concerts. Bloom's off the rose. Why do you think I book us for so many concerts?"

"Bloom off the rose. Yeah, well we'll see about that," came the reply. "Well, I will. You sure won't."

Charlie was beginning to feel weak from the loss of blood from two bullet wounds and getting banged up in the crash. "You forgot one thing," he said. "My body. The cops will see my bullet wounds. They're not entirely stupid."

"Nope. I got it covered. You'll see. Come to think of it, no. No, you won't. You'll be deader than Ricky Nelson. And I'll be spending all your money. Not you."

"That's cold. Deep space, dark side of the moon cold," said Blind Charlie.

Watts had nothing more to say about that.

The fire crackled in the barn. Snow continued to fall. About an inch had blanketed Charlie's chest. When he tried to brush it off his arms it hurt too much for the effort. So Charlie just lay there plotting the revenge he would wreak on Watts once they got back to civilization. He would see to it that he would never work as a musician again.

Mike Watts seemed oblivious to having just been in a plane crash to say nothing of shooting his best friend. He drifted off to sleep dreaming of all the ways he would be spending millions of dollars on a Bel Air mansion, drugs, booze and broads. And a bright, red, Lamborghini Coontach. He reveled in his dream world.

After a while, sitting in solitude, Charlie allowed for the fact he might actually die either from injuries sustained in the crash or from Watt's puny gun. With that thought fixed in mind he determinedly began to crawl towards the approximate location where he had last heard Mike Watt's voice and the sound of gunshots.

Chapter Six

The fire raged. Then died.

Two long days later, the wicked storm broke, the sky cleared, the stars in the Milky Way galaxy twinkled brightly, and the temperature plummeted from the upper teens to below zero. A pack of snowmobilers on a midnight joyride with their wives were enjoying the spectacle of freshly fallen snow reflecting pure white under the glimmering full moon. It was a magical winter wonderland made warmer with judicious sips of Apple Jack from a shared hip flask. That is until the two couples happened upon the crash site.

From a distance, the snowmobilers thought they were approaching a barn fire that had fizzled out and was reduced to dying embers giving off thin wisps of smoke, a more noxious smell than smoke.

The snowmobilers were familiar with this notorious, abandoned farm and its local legends. Decades before, the property's dimwitted owner, Edgar Hill, used to deliver bales of hay to his pastured milk cows in the cargo bed of his collision-damaged 1936 Rolls Royce Phantom that he had cut down into a pickup truck. The nearly worn-out Rolls V-12 engine burned so much oil the tailpipe smoked like a stove burning damp, green wood. No big surprise, Edgar bought cheap 30-weight oil by the case.

In town, around the pickle barrel at the Buggy Whip general store, old-timers used to drink coffee and take cruel delight in poking fun at Edgar Hill and his strange ways. Especially his chopped Rolls, which they mockingly referred to as Agnes, appropriately named after the Rolls pickup truck made famous in the old Travis

McGee detective novels.

"Drink Plymouth Gin, too, do ya', Edgar," they would tease. Another literary allusion lost on Edgar, who couldn't read and didn't know who author John D. MacDonald was.

"Got any big salvage cases you're working on?"

"How's the weather in the marina down there in Fort Lauderdale?"

The old-timers were nothing less than senior citizen bullies who should have been ashamed of themselves. But they weren't. Instead, they fancied themselves as brilliant satirists.

Back in those days, Edgar had worked his 110-acre dairy farm with his siblings, brother Wilbur and sister Effie Mae. Besides a modestly-sized herd of Guernseys, the cow barn sheltered several workhorses. The stable's dirt floor, bedded with straw, fouled straw the Hill brothers never bothered to turn with a pitchfork.

Then there was the nasty rumor that Effie Mae was Wilbur's mother. And that Effie Mae's father was also Wilbur and Edgar's father. But that's a story for another time. That and the story of Edgar's trial on weapons charges and his disappearance from the face of the earth.

When the snowmobilers drew closer to the Old Hill Farm, they saw the rear stabilizer of Dangerous Dave's wrecked plane dangling high up in the branches of a pine tree like an over-sized Christmas ornament. They drew a little closer, yet they saw two bodies laid out in the snow alongside each other. Having heard on the news how a plane had been missing for a few days, seeing the smoking barn and then finding two men laid out on the ground, they had quickly surmised the tragedy they had stumbled upon.

Snowmachine engines idling, the couples climbed off the padded touring seats with the good intentions of rendering aid and assistance. One of the wives, Nancy, was an RN, an emergency room nurse. Clad in bulky thermal coveralls and a ski mask her husband Maynard had given her for Christmas, Nurse Nancy tromped over through the snow to triage the two poor souls.

Most folks, when faced with dead bodies, are shocked and upset. But not Nancy, or her husband, Maynard. She was used to it from her time staffing the Emergency Room. She wasn't afraid of anything.

Neither was her husband, Maynard. As for Maynard, well, let's just say Maynard had deployed, had gone to war.

Nancy found one man alive and barely conscious. Likely suffering from exposure and damage to his internal organs from the impact of the airplane coming to an abrupt stop, she surmised. From the characteristic stink of a hospital urinal emanating from the victim's clothes, she presumed him to be laying in a puddle of his own frozen urine. She further diagnosed he had ruptured his bladder in the crash.

Her husband, Maynard Reece, a hunting guide, had walked up to the burned-out barn and peered inside, knowing what he would find. The stench of burned bodies hung thick in the frigid winter air. He knew the stink quite well from his experiences in another time and place.

With his Special Forces Commando LED flashlight, he shined a pencil-thin beam of light on the wreckage inside of the burned-to-the-ground barn.

Not good, he thought.

"Looks like there might be more of them in there," he called out, choking on lingering smoke. Maynard could taste the foul smell of the burned bodies on his tongue. He wanted to go inside to see if he could do anything for the poor souls but was afraid the wreckage would collapse on top of him. Besides, they were likely goners. Rather wisely, he walked away, going over to see if he could help his wife.

The other victim laying at Nurse Nancy's feet was dead and looked as if he had been for some time. Blind Charlie was as stiff as a 2 x 8 pine plank and not rigor mortis. Instead, his corpse was frozen solid from exposure to the elements, his skin a ghoulish white, the grimaced lips heart-attack blue. His front teeth were showing. White guy overbite, she mused.

Upon closer examination, Nurse Nancy noticed that not only was he not wearing a jacket, the sleeves of his flannel shirt looked like they had been ripped away. Both arms looked like they had been gnawed clean to the bone by a wild animal. Or something. "Oh, my, God," she uttered.

There was lots of blood splattered on the snow around the corpse. Illuminated by the full moon, in sharp contrast to the pure white snow, blood splatter around the body looked black in the darkness. Nurse Nancy could taste the coppery smell of the blood in her mouth. Assessing the crash site, she predicted the autopsy reports for all the dead would likely read: Cause of Death: Blunt Force Trauma.

"But what of the horrific injuries to his arms? Did the plane crash do that?" she wondered.

Nancy went back to the first victim, the one she would later learn was Mike Watts, the supergroup's legendary drummer. This time she noticed how his face and hair caked in frozen blood. Strangely, there didn't appear to be any lacerations on his body. So where did the blood come from, she wondered?

Coming to consciousness, Watts's eyelids flickered open. "You, my angel?" he asked weakly.

"Oh, good. You're alive." Nurse Nancy noticed a faint trickle of dried blood in the corners of his mouth. Inside his mouth, she saw what looked like torn shreds of raw, red meat stuck between his teeth and gums. His breath stunk.

One of the other snowmobilers found a signal on her cellphone and called the state troopers.

Chapter Seven

Officers Thorndike and Barnhardt showed up in their All Wheel Drive SUV cruiser at the crash site and were soon busily stringing yellow crime scene tape around the perimeter.

Detective Kurt Donner shivered from the intense cold, rubbing his gloved hands together, cupping them, breathing warm air onto his stiff fingers. He repeatedly stomped his LL Bean boots hard on the snow-packed ground, trying to restore feeling to his toes gone numb in the below zero temperature.

He did not like cold, which he associated with death, specifically his own death, the notion of eternity, the infinity of space. Emptiness. Mortality. A topic that should probably be covered in a future session with his PTSD psychiatrist, he mused,

The smell from the burnt bodies was horrible, overpowering. An odor once experienced that can never be put out of your mind. Rationally, logically, the smell being reminiscent of a backyard barbecue shouldn't bother the human soul. Thinking about what the smell meant works horrors in the darkest corners of one's mind.

Even worse than the psychological impact of being exposed to the smell, the odor saturates deep to the molecular levels in the fibers of your clothes. A stink that can never be laundered clean no matter how many wash cycles or jugs of detergent and boxes of Borax are dumped in the wash water. The pungent smell from a startled skunk can be deodorized by bathing a hairy pet in a solution of tomato juice and vinegar. But the concoction does nothing tangible for the smell of a burned corpse.

The acrid smell is eternal. It lives forever. The only recourse is to consign the offensive coat, pants, shirt, underwear, socks, and shoes, the lot, to the dumpster. Or, ironically, to burn them in a roaring bonfire.

From experience at crime scenes and car accidents, the EMTs on the scene knew precisely what to do. Before they left their station, they had rather wisely first donned white, Tyvek suits and booties.

So too had the wrecker driver, Big Tim, prepared in the same garb. Big Tim had attended too many car wrecks where vehicles had burned to a crisp, driver and passengers buckled inside, unable to escape the inferno because their seat belt buckles had jammed. Or because horrible injuries left them too weak to escape. They just sat helplessly screaming at the top of their lungs while fire broiled them alive.

"Buckle Up For Safety, Buckle Up!" Tim scoffed, "Yeah, right." At crash scenes, hearing motorists scream in agony, burning to death, was why Big Tim never buckled up. He did not want his body to end up in char city, burning to death, screaming in agony at the top of his lungs. Sometimes nightmares woke him up in the wee hours, his heart racing his throat raw from screaming. No, sir. No seat belts.

Chapter Eight

This was not the first time Detective Donner had been on the property. Years before, when he had been a young copper just out of the police academy, there had been a house fire. Effie Mae had been deep-frying doughnuts in a black, cast-iron frying pan filled with hot, bubbling corn oil. Feeble-minded, Effie Mae had been careless, and the hot oil had burst into flames catching her frilly window curtains on fire. Pity, she had hand-sewn them
herself.

Hearts racing, Effie Mae and her two brothers, Edgar and Wilbur, had rather wisely evacuated the wood frame home post-haste, escaping injury.

The cops and fire department showed up on the scene promptly enough.

Edgar histrionically ran back and forth in the front yard, yelling and screaming, pleading for the firefighters to go into the burning building with him to save his precious gun collection.

They did.

The following day the Shiretown Standard's front page showed pictures of firefighters running out the front door of the Hill home cradling armfuls of old, military surplus rifles.

As the old-timers at the Buggy Whip like to tell the story, there were dozens and dozens of French Lebels, German Mausers, and 1903 Springfield rifles. The Hill home had been like an armory. One picture showed a close-up of Gorman, the big, fat fire chief, with a mile-wide grin on his face, cradling a Thompson submachine gun replete with a 50-round drum. It turned out the Tommy gun was loaded.

In the middle of the firearms recovery, Wilbur nonchalantly asked could the firefighters also grab the two cases of dynamite from down in the basement along with all the tracer and armor-piercing ammunition and hand grenades.

Gorman shrieked. "Did he say dynamite! Everybody out! Now!" Eyes wide like a cat, dropping the Thompson in the grass, Gorman waddled for the safety of the treeline a hundred yards away.

The most dramatic of the Shiretown Standard's front page photos showed the Hill house a fraction of a second after 100 pounds of 60% dynamite detonated. That particular photo broadcast on TV and later introduced as evidence at trial showed a massive cloud of smoke and bits of roofing tile and wood splinters being hurling high into the heavens. The blast was so loud it was heard miles away in Burlington. Some claim it rattled windows across the border in Canada.

Witness testimony revealed how an estimated 100 thousand rounds of high-powered rifle ammo cooked off in the burning embers one, two, and three rounds at a time: Pew. Pew-pew. Pew-pew-pew, for hours after the fire proper had been extinguished.

There was a trial.

There was a guilty verdict.

Out on bail, neither Edgar, Wilbur, or Effie Mae showed up for sentencing. The trio disappeared into the night, presumed to have fled the jurisdiction, never to be heard from again. Because Agnes, Edgar's Rolls Royce pickup conversion, had also disappeared, the three co-defendants were have presumed to have made their getaway in her. Running for parts unknown.

An All Points Bulletin was summarily issued, but the trio was never seen again. It was as if they had disappeared from the face of the earth.

Time passed.

Eventually, Donner added mightily to his firearms collection. With Edgar Hill, a felon on the run, his guns were up for grabs. His weapons held in the evidence locker were sold at auction, Donner won the bid.

Sometimes on weekends, Donner shot the Thompson when he could afford the exorbitant cost of the Full Metal Jacket 45 ACP ammo. With a 50-round drum, it didn't take long to burn through a week's pay worth of ammunition on full automatic.

Donner chuckled in remembrance of the ear-shattering explosion at the Hill farmstead. Years later, his ear still rang from the concussion. Looking over to where the Hill house had once stood, he continued he gazed at the burned-out barn with the crashed and burned plane inside.

Chapter Nine

By mid-morning, Nurse Nancy, her husband Maynard, and their two friends, had calmly told their stories to the cops, been patted on the head for their care and concern, and then sent home on their snow machines. Presumably, it was a long ride home sans loud whooping and hollering.

An Air Ambulance helicopter had landed on the makeshift Landing Zone to ferry Mike Watts to the intensive care unit at the university hospital. At the same time, EMTs had zipped up Blind Charlie into a black body bag. They had tasked the Bell helicopter with delivering the frozen corpse to the coroner's office for what was presumed would be an interesting autopsy. At least once, Blind Charlie's corpse thawed to room temperature.

All three dead bodies were recovered from the wreckage inside the barn. At least, what was left of them. Most of the gray-white ashes, blackened bits of bone, and wallets had been scooped into brown paper grocery sacks and transported into town by the Graves Funeral Home hearse.

The on-the-scene FAA investigator had yet to figure out how to extract what was left of the fuselage from the barn. Its aluminum-magnesium alloy skin had ignited, burning white-hot. Generating heat as intense as a thermite flare, the fuselage self-consumed at a temperature of 4,000 degrees Fahrenheit. Literally burning itself to the ground, it left a pan with human ashes and bones concentrated in three neat little piles.

Which particular ashes and bone fragments belonged to

which specific person would be sorted at a later date, perhaps by lottery. Three dead guys, ten pounds of human ashes, and bones equaled two or three pounds per family. One generous scoop of human remains for you, and another for you, thank you very much. And one more scoop of gray ashes for this guy too.

The clean-up crew hired by the county had yanked the rear stabilizer down out of the tree and loaded it and both wings onto the cargo bed of a flatbed truck.]

Detective Donner was amazed to learn from Big Tim that the Pratt and Whitney and its propeller had survived virtually intact. Big Tim was busy stringing a length of wire rope into the depths of the burned-out barn with plans to winch the radial engine out of the wreckage.

Once recovered, all the Beaver parts were destined to be reassembled in a hangar by FAA investigators in an attempt to find out the cause of the crash. Human error or mechanical failure. But even this early in the investigation, there didn't seem to be any doubt as to what had gone so horribly wrong.

"If past proves to be prologue," the FAA investigator told Detective Donner, "In about a year, NTSB will conclude pilot error. May his eternal soul rest in peace. He stupidly took off in a storm against FAA advice. Bad weather caused the wings to ice over, at which point they stopped providing lift, the plane stopped flying, crashed to the ground, and burned. Four the people dead, end of story. So sorry."

Donner made a feeble attempt at gallows humour, "So what you're telling me is that it wasn't the fall that killed these guys. It was the sudden stop." He thought he was being funny.

The FAA guy groaned. "Gee. That's the first time I heard that one. Not." He turned his back on Donner and
walked away, shaking his head in judgment.

A few yards from the charred barn and airplane wreckage, the prerequisite yellow barricade tape with prominent black, block letters warned:

Police Line - Do Not Cross!

Officers Thorndike and Barnes had strung barricade tape outlining the location where Mike Watt's had been found lying alongside Blind Charlie's body.

"Kinda like the streets of the city, white chalk outline on a sidewalk around a dead Boston mobster," mused Big Tim. A couple of years before, he had retired to the Berkshires from Roxbury.

Detective Kurt Donner, or Donny, as he was disrespectfully called behind his back by peers, was not well-liked by any of the other cops in his department. Or for that matter, by anyone in the environs of Shiretown, Vermont. Not even his current wife (Mrs. Donner number 3), or his daughter, Lena Marie, liked him.

Notoriously, early on in his career, Donner had checked out every one of the books in the city library that he deemed subversive and burned the bunch of them in a big, roaring bonfire in his back yard. When the library sent notice of fines for the overdue books, he burned them too. He refused to pay. Suffice it to say. He no longer had a library card. He was not liked there either.

Donner owned an impressive gun collection. Naturally, some of the weapons were appropriated from crime scenes. Others were notorious, infamous. Like his prized possession: A once-fired .38-caliber Colt snub nose revolver used by a distraught blonde who had allegedly killed herself with a single gunshot to the temple after finding out her boyfriend had cheated on her.

Permanent solution.

Temporary problem.

Poor dead, Linda Allay.

Once released from evidence, Donner had bought the

revolver from Linda's father for his collection. Once in his possession, Donner archived the suicide Colt on the top shelf of his gun safely, tucked inside its original factory box, replete with the original blood-stained, price tag hanging from the trigger guard by its little white string. The blued finish was deeply rusted from the acidic splatter of Linda's blood and brains, damage done while it sat uncleaned in the evidence locker awaiting trial.

Whenever Donner took the Colt out of the safe and held it in his hand, he could feel evil and death emanating from it to the depths of his soul. Linda's case, and the dreadful set of emotions he felt whenever holding the revolver, reminded him of why he found catharsis in solving homicides.

But I digress. Suffice it to say. Donner was an avid firearms aficionado. Yet, hypocritically, he could often be heard spouting off on his soapbox, ranting and raving that nobody but cops should be allowed to own firearms, handguns, and semi-automatic rifles - especially .38 caliber snub-nose revolvers.

In his 20 years with the Shiretown PD, he had been involved in a couple of shootings, duly investigated, and ultimately deemed justifiable. Even the ones where he had killed the perps: Two in the chest and one right between the eyes. One of them had been Linda's so-called boyfriend. The evil sumbitch had needed killing.

When his boss ordered Donner to seek counseling for PTSD, the psychiatrist diagnosed him as not suffering from PTSD but rather from being a first-rate asshole.

Social pariah, yes. But as a detective, solving cases that left other detectives befuddled, he did very well, principally due to his diligence and unwavering attention to detail. Donner wasn't particularly smart. His big shame in life was that he had miserably failed the test to get on the Vermont State Patrol.

But investigating a case in his jurisdiction, he never let
go, not in Linda's murder and not in the instant case that
would come to focus on Michael John Watts as the prime
suspect.

Donner walked the length and breadth of the crime
scene, thinking about what he knew so far. A plane crash,
he mused. His shrink would call it an incident.

Donner walked the perimeter again, walking and
thinking and then thinking some more. Before the EMTs
had zipped Blind Charlie into the body bag, he had
perfunctorily examined the ravaged arms. And he had
talked to Nurse Nancy, listening to her cite her credentials
as a trauma nurse. And what she said, she thought she had
seen stuck between Watts' teeth.

"Macabre," she had called it.

"Evidence," is what Donner had called it.

Chapter Ten

The Shiretown Standard headline was scandalously graphic, which, no big surprise, sold lots of papers. Sex sells but nowhere nearly as well as a tale of cannibalism. Besides selling out at the newsstand, the website lit up like a church on Sunday with a plethora of ghoulish visitors from around the world.

Rocker Plane Crashes

Cannibal Band Member only Survivor

In graphic detail, the reporter explained how after takeoff, the de Havilland wings had iced over, causing the plane to go into an aerodynamic stall, crash into the side of a barn and burn to a crisp incinerating the pilot and passengers. The writer told how it had been two days before authorities could find the crash site. This was for the simple reason the pilot had failed to file a flight plan, complicated in no small part by a wicked storm dumping a plethora of snow on the countryside from the Canadian border all the way south to Virginia.

Even more outrageous than the pilot's negligence was that while waiting to be rescued, one of the surviving band members, the drummer, had consumed both arms of the band's namesake, Blind Charlie. Ostensibly he committed this barbaric act to prevent starving to death.

The article went on to recount a similar occurrence in 1846 with the infamous Donner Party when pioneers who had set out for California in a wagon train became snowbound in the Sierra Nevada and resorted to cannibalism to stay alive.

There was also the haunting tale of a Rugby team

crashing high in the Andes Mountains, waiting 72 days on the side of a mountain for rescue. They, too, resorted to cannibalism to survive.

Just the day before in Vatican City, Pope Albert, hearing of the Shiretown crash, decreed according to church doctrine that Mike Watts had committed no sin by eating the flesh of his dead friend. Body of Christ and all that.

No big surprise Rolling Stone ran a stop-the-presses obituary, detailing how coincidentally Blind Charlie had grown up in Hibbing, Minnesota, just a couple of doors down the street from Robert Alan Zimmerman, aka, Bob Dylan. And how Blind Charlie's Corner, the Super Group, had been named after Blind Charlie himself.

The story related how Charlie used to set up in Harvard Square and play his heart out for spare change as an aspiring musician. His guitar case, spread wide open on the sidewalk beside him, was accompanied by a placard proclaiming:

Blind Charlie's Corner

Eventually, Charlie outgrew busking, formed Blind Charlie's Corner, and began to play the Cambridge club scene like Club Passim's and Keith Dempster's Coffee Mill. The rest was, as Rolling Stone commented, Rock and Roll history.

Of course, the Standard's obituary dutifully recited the litany of all the dead boys in the band. In particular, Alan Lage, vocalist, who stuttered except when he sang on stage, was famous for predicting Blind Charlie's music was destined to save the world with Rock and Roll.

Indeed, the entire world would mourn the loss of Blind Charlie's music.

Chapter Eleven

The county attorney was a lethargic bum, a lazy lawyer who pressed defendant clients for plea bargains so he wouldn't have to prepare for trial.

Back in the day when he was still a bartender at the George's, a local watering hole, 55-year old Klaus Dickner had visited the SocialSecurity.gov website to determine how much money he would be entitled to after retirement.

The news was not good.

For many years Dickner had neglected to declare, let alone pay, a whit of Federal taxes on his tips. So it should have come as no big surprise for him to learn his projected social security check would not be enough for him to afford even being homeless in retirement.

Salvation, he figured, would be found in getting a higher paying job and dutifully paying taxes for the next ten or twelve years, which would kick him up into a higher benefits bracket. With that strategy in mind, he considered the options: Become a nurse, a postman, a lawyer.

Work the system.

Do whatever it took.

Dickner settled on becoming a brother of the blood, keeping his night job as a bartender and working his way through law school. From that day on, he dutifully declared all of his tips to the IRS.

Studying in the law library, the young baby snakes, as he called the law students, mistakenly believed the poorly dressed, unkempt, albeit more mature man to be a wizened, criminal defense lawyer researching case law.

He never bothered to enlighten them.

Which meant he did pretty well with the young Sally coeds, which further meant his grades suffered. Graduating at the rock bottom of his class and barely passing the bar exam in four attempts (The max allowed), there were no offers from any law firms, not even the mom and pop shops. So he took the only job he could get as Waxahatchie County attorney in Shiretown, Vermont. The salary was modest, benefits adequate, and there was a retirement plan. It would do fine until he retired in a few years. Until then, Dickner was marking time.

Dickner was debating Donner on the merits of the instant case. "Yeah, but what crime do you allege Watts committed? Most days, I could indict a ham sandwich, but I don't think I have enough evidence to indict Watts. And then there's public opinion. He's even got that crazy pontiff on his side. It's good to have friends in high places."

"For starters, charge him with desecration of a corpse," suggested Donner.

"Can you prove it? You've already told me he ate the evidence."

"On its face, that's tampering with evidence, a felony. Or did you miss that class in law school? And the mutilated corpse is evidence enough."

Donner methodically ticked off the critical elements of the alleged crime. "Blind Charlie's arms chewed off. Human flesh stuck in Watts' teeth. DNA testing will prove it belongs to Blind Charlie. And the kicker, Watts, admitted that he did it! We have his bedside confession to the newspapers."

"Mens rhea, "commented Dickner. "Criminal intent. If he did it to avoid starving to death, there was no criminal intent. No crime committed."

"Starving to death. You've got to be kidding. Watts was only out there two days!"

Dickner countered with a salient rebuttal. "Watts didn't have a knife, so how did he carve the meat off? Gnaw like a beaver?"

"As a matter of fact. Yes, he did. Were you not listening? They found human flesh stuck in his gums. Charlie's bones show scoring from human teeth."

"DNA test results back yet?"

Donner shrugged. "No. Not yet anyway."

"Didn't think so. Besides, Watts is on record as being a vegan. Don't you read Rolling Stone? Something about seeing his grandmother slaughter chickens on the family farm when he was just a tow-headed kid back in North Carolina."

The detective was thinking aloud, "Okay, another angle. So let's say he didn't eat his friend. What if he just wanted to spoof us into thinking he did."

"Spoof?"

"Okay, devil's advocate, for the sake of argument," said Dickner. "Let's say Watts didn't consume the flesh? Then where's the flesh that's missing from the arms? Using the Rules of Nines doctors use to assess the percentage of burn on burn unit victims, I figure six pounds of meat are missing from Charlie's arms. That's a lot of meat." He corrected himself, "Human flesh. And he'd still need a knife to get at it, wouldn't he? He hide it somewhere around the crash site? "

Donner palmed his face in frustration. "His leg broken. He couldn't walk to the barn and throw evidence in the fire. There was no knife. Autopsy would have shown if there had been. Blade would have left marks on the bones. Coroner reports teeth marks, not knife scoring."

Dickner threw his hands up. "Whatever. Trying to

help."

Detective Donner said, "What bothers me most was the fact that Michael John Watts had only been out in the woods for two days waiting to be rescued. So how could his hunger grow so intense in such a short time?"

Dickner said nothing.

"I don't buy it," said Donner.

The two men sat in their chairs, glaring at each other.

Donner finally said, "I'm going back out to the crash site."

"By the way, I've been meaning to ask," said Dickner, snickering. "You find it ironic you of all people are investigating this case? I mean. Donner. You know. The Donner party?"

"Dickner," said the detective in a monotone.

"What?"

"Bite me. No pun intended."

Chapter Twelve

Spring was in the air, a bright, bright sunshiny day. All the snow had melted. By now, the fire had grown cold. No longer smoldering like a blacksmith's forge, there was no smoke, the air was clean to breathe again. Most of the wreckage had been dragged away. Only the debris of the burned-out barn stood in silent testimony to the tragedy. Ribbons of yellow and black barricade tape were still in place, fluttering in the light breeze. Biodegradable, they would soon be gone.

Donner was once again on-premises, walking the perimeter of the crash site, trying to make sense of what he knew.

A flock of ten to twenty blackbirds, wary of the intruder's presence, perched in pine trees jabbering away with each other: Caw, caw, cawing.

If only the crows could talk, mused Donner, maybe the birds would tell him what had really gone on that fearful night.

At the top of the hill, he spotted a couple of crows down on the ground, hopping around, picking away at some dead animal. Probably eating the guts out of a dead squirrel, he reckoned, walking uphill to see what it was. Predictably, as soon as he got within a few feet of the carcass, the birds flew off.

He could see they had been gorging on a dead, bloody rabbit. "Damn crows will eat anything," he muttered. "Just like damn Watts . . ."

He hunkered down on the wet ground, mindful to keep

his butt dry, looking around the area cordoned off by caution tape. Just looking and thinking. He did not know what he was looking for but would know it when he found it. Over by where Blind Charlie had been found in macabre repose, the

crows were going at it again: Caw, caw, caw. One crow swooped in low to the ground, landed, and started pecking at something shiny, sparkling in the sunlight.

Dutifully Donner got to his feet then walked towards the sparkle. Once again, when he got too close, the crow flew away. Donner lifted the caution tape and stepped beneath it. And then he could see what had attracted the crow's interest. "Hot damn," was his excited utterance.

The sparkle in the sunlight turned out to be a diminutive, spent cartridge case, caliber .25 ACP. Only slightly tarnished from the weather, it had not been exposed to the elements long enough for the weather to dull its brass surface. Curiously, it was the same caliber as the Raven pistol found in Watt's jacket pocket along with his cellphone.

Donner poked around, hoping to find another spent cartridge case in close proximity. Jiggling the empty shell casing in the palm of his hand, he pondered how the Raven they had recovered from Watts was a six-shot, semi-automatic pistol and how it had been found with three live rounds in the magazine and one in the chamber, four rounds in all.

"Do the math," he mused. Six-round capacity, minus the four live rounds, equals two fired. Minus the one in his hand. So naturally, it followed there should be one more empty cartridge case lying around somewhere on the ground at his feet. He looked in vain but never did find it. He thought that circumstance to be intriguing.

But even more intriguing was the fired casing he had recovered.

Chapter Thirteen

Another bright, bright sunshiny day, about a month after the plane crash, lilac buds were beginning to sprout. In a week's time, they would reveal themselves as brilliant, purple blossoms, likely just in time for Easter Sunday.

After his breakfast of coffee and a slab of Georgia Peach pie at Rosie's, Detective Donner was back at the hospital with the mission of re-interviewing a still-recovering Mike Watts. His leg had indeed been broken but was healing. X-rays showed a green-stick-fractured tibia along with several broken ribs on the left side of his body. Donner thought it entirely appropriate that a pine tree had broken his fall when Watts had been thrown from the plane, thereby preventing him from a soft landing in a snowbank. Karma, sweet karma, he mused.

Standing by the side of Watts' hospital bed, Detective Donner forced a smile and made eye contact. Donner known for his pathetic smile, so forced, so twisted, that some of his fellow Shiretown officers joked it could curdle milk.

Donner smiled at Watts.

"Ossifer," yawned a just waking up Watts, intentionally mispronouncing the word officer as a show of disrespect for men in blue. With his long history of misdemeanor arrests for simple possession of marijuana, Watts did not like cops, judges, or lawyers.

"Detective," corrected Donner. "I'm a detective, not an officer. And certainly not an ossifer."

"Whatever," said Watts, rolling his eyes as if he cared.

Donner went on, bluntly asking, "Mr. Watts, want to tell me why you Googled the Donner Party and the Andes flight disaster while stranded in the woods with Blind Charlie?"

Watts did not respond. So that's why they seized his cell phone, he mused. Maybe he should ask for a lawyer. It also worried him that they had taken his beloved Raven pistol.

"Ya got me. I Googled cannibalism. DNA will confirm I ate my friend's arm. So what? Under the circumstances, isn't a jury in the world that'll convict me. Even Pope Albert over there in Rome has taken my side."

"I suspect there's more to it than that," said Donner. "Tell me, why it is you never thought to call someone to rescue you? Too wrapped up in your online research? Your phone has GPS. We know you knew exactly where you were. You plotted it on MapQuest. So why did you want to stay out there in the wilderness when you could have come home at any time?"

Watts did not respond. Yeah, I'm probably going to need a lawyer, he thought.

"And how is it you got so bloody hungry in just two days, so ravenously hungry, you felt compelled to gnaw Charlie's arm down to the bone?"

Donner reached into his vest pocket, pulled out a folded sheet of paper, and laid it with exaggerated care on Watt's lap.

Watts thought it looked official, like a report of some kind. A cold shiver ran up and down his spine. He did not want to pick up the paper, let alone unfold it and find out what it had to say.

Donner pointed to the paper. "Pathology report. When Doctor Drevyanko examined the humerus bones on Charlie's corpse, he found microscopic traces of copper and lead smeared on both of them. You know, bullet metal. From a slug."

Donner paused for effect before going on. "You wanna explain that little coincidence?"

Once again, Watts failed to respond.

He just peed the bed. Annoyingly, he had been incontinent of bladder ever since the crash, and the condition worsened whenever he felt nervous.

Donner was using a modified version of the Reid interview technique, flat out telling his suspect the results of his investigation that indicated he had committed the crime in question. Donner was not the least bit concerned about eliciting a false confession from Watts when he said, "I figure you shot Charlie to bleed him to death, then tried to cover the crime by eating the evidence."

For a brief moment, Watts furrowed his brow in worried disbelief, then recovered and began gesturing, circling his finger near his temple. "You're as cracked as a porcelain piss pot, officer." This time he had correctly pronounced the word officer. "Why would I do such a thing? We're Blind Charlie's Corner. Not those freaks KISS biting the heads off live chickens."

Donner chuckled, "I know what you're thinking, and it doesn't matter one whit that we don't have the slugs."

Donner was deep in his element. He liked drama. He especially liked using the Reid technique to unnerve perpetrators. A higher court judge had once confided to Donner that whenever a defendant was losing at trial, he would grant every objection his lawyer made, not wanting to lend any grounds for appeal after having been found guilty. Kind of like the axiom suggesting one should never interrupt an enemy in the midst of making a fool of himself.

Donner reached into his jacket pocket, pulling out yet another piece of evidence, it too in a clear, plastic bag. He held it up for Watts to see, giving the bag a couple of shakes for dramatic effect.

Inside it, Watts saw a single, brass cartridge case. He recognized it. He gulped.

Donner broke a smile at Watt's worried reaction, telling him, "We don't have the slugs, but we do have fired cases from your Raven. Coroner found this one lodged in Blind Charlie's mouth between his tongue and cheek. Caliber .25 Automatic Cartridge Pistol. Same caliber as the .25 Raven pistol emergency room personnel found in your coat pocket. Registered to you. Coroner missed this shell casing the first time around."

Donner pulled out a second evidence baggy, this time with the spent casing he had found at the crash site. "Also .25 ACP. When I found it at the crash site, I asked the coroner to look at the cadaver one more time, only with more scrutiny. That's when he found the lead smears on the bones and the second cartridge case wedged in Charlie's mouth."

He shook both baggies for effect.

Watts squirmed.

"We fired your piece-of-junk pistol in the state's ballistics lab." Donner shook his head in disgust. "Come on, man. A Raven? New Orleans pimp gun? Chrome plated. Pearl handled grips. With all your money, you couldn't afford a couple hundred bucks more for a decent pistol? Not even a High Point? That's embarrassing."

He went on, "Back when we had hope of finding one of the projectiles you fired into Charlie's arms, our tech fired four rounds into ballistic gelatin. He set aside the fired bullets as evidence. Next, he examined the empties under a stereomicroscope. Markings on the sides of the shell casings and the imprint made by the extractor on the rim are a perfect match for the casing we recovered from inside Charlie's mouth. That means your POS Raven fired the cartridge case in Charlie's mouth and the one in the grass at the crash site. Oh, and those four unfired rounds in your coat pocket. Same brand head stamped on the casing in Charlie's mouth and the one in the grass."

Donner shook both bags in unison.

"You don't understand," burbled Watts. "Yes, I admit I shot him for target practice. But he was already dead. I was bored. No, wait, I was out of my mind. Besides. What's the harm?"

"Am I to understand your story is that Charlie was killed in the crash."

"Yeah,

"Already dead?"

"Yes."

"So that's your story, and you're sticking to it?"

"Yes! Gospel truth."

"Let you in on a secret." Donner nodded commiseratively, "Gospel truth. Corpses don't bleed. Think it's in the bible. The one you just quoted."

Watts said, "Uh..."

Donner said, matter-of-factly. "All that blood in the snow around Charlie's body. If he died in the crash, where did all the blood come from?"

"Uh. Dunno" shrugged Watts.

"I do. He exsanguinated. Fancy word in the coroner's report for Charlie bleeding to death from a gunshot wound. Doctor Drevyanko says Charlie likely would have survived his injuries from the crash if you hadn't shot him. Death Certificate is going to read: Cause of Death: Gunshot Wounds."

Donner was lying, more Reid method. The fact of the matter is that corpses do sometimes bleed after death and dying, depending on the circumstances.

Donner waved a finger in Michael John Watts' face, "I charge you, Michael John Watts, with First-degree murder. And your good friend, Blind Charlie, reached up from the grave to point an accusing finger at you, condemning you to death."

He shook the evidence bags again, saying in monotone, "Your Death Certificate is going to say Cause of Death: Lethal Injection."

Chapter Fourteen

Given the mountain of evidence Donner assembled against Watts, the ultimate outcome was as certain as the sea is salt. Even for fumbling Dickner, it was a cakewalk: A conviction. The jury had come back with its verdict for capital punishment before lunch.

Michael John Watts would own the distinction of being the first prisoner given a death sentence in decades. Capital punishment had been abolished in 1972. Vermont had last executed a prisoner in 1954 when Donald DeMag was put to death for the double robbery murder he had committed after escaping while serving a life sentence for an earlier murder.

Like folks are fond of saying down in the Great State of Texas, DeMag needed killing.

Unlucky for Watts, the State of Vermont had re-instituted capital punishment just a couple of months before the plane crash and Blind Charlie's grotesque murder, making Watts eligible for a death sentence.

Punishment loomed.

Just not right away.

Behind bars for years, first awaiting trial and then after the guilty verdict, exhausting all of his appeals, had lent John Michael Watts copious time to think.

To think about stuff.

Just stuff.

In his copious free time behind bars, he remembered a John Candy movie. In it, a guy on vacation in the Great North Woods gorged himself on a huge beef steak. His man versus meat victory won a free meal for himself and his family plus a fire engine red T-shirt proclaiming:

I ate a 96er!

The infamous Ole 96er, six pounds of meat, gristle, and fat.

No longer a vegetarian after a couple of years in

 the joint, the raucous Hollywood movie had inspired Watts' choice for his special meal, his last meal on earth.

Besides watching movies, Watts also reflected on his childhood memories of growing up on the family farm near Elbow Lick, North Carolina. Remembering grandma Madge and her billowing, white apron brought him joy. She used to bring him along to the chicken coop to gather eggs from her flock of cackling, bitty hens. "Dumb clucks," she used to call them.

Watts chuckled fondly in remembrance.

He also remembered long, hot summers on the farm, sitting on the porch with grandpa Morse and grandma Madge, waiting for the sun to go down when the temperature would be cool enough to go to sleep.

Grandpa and grandma Krempaski, his mother's parents, were DPs, Displaced Persons, Polish refugees from the Second World War in Europe. No big surprise, they spoke with accents so thick you could cut their words apart with a hatchet.

Watts fondly remembered helping grandma Madge pick Red Ripper field peas, dumping the harvest of pods into a burlap bag, and whamming the side of the bag with a big stick. Afterward, she would scoop a handful of shucked peas, patiently emptying them into a bucket, letting the breeze winnow away the chaff while they fell.

Foremost in his memories of grandma Krempaski was the fateful Sunday morning when she had taken him by the hand and led him out to the barnyard, saying gruffly, "You're a big boy now, plenty old enough to see this."

With her billowing white apron grandma, Madge shooed a red rooster into a corner of the chicken pen, roughly grabbed the bird by the neck, dragged him over to the chopping block, and lopped off his head with a hatchet.

One whack.

Feathers flew.

Blood spurted.

She explained while the headless rooster danced around like a chicken with his head cut off. "Been a troublemaker lately. Pissed me off. Now go play."

Suppertime, Grandma called young Michael Watts to the dinner table for a feast of chicken and homemade egg noodles. Unable to put his fork down, he remembered it as the best bird he had ever eaten. Eating a second helping of the home cooking, he washed it down with a big glass of lime green Kool-Aid garnished with slices of orange.

Not until years later did he realize where the chicken had come from. Trouble making rooster, dumb sumbitch.

Don't ever piss off grandma was the lesson learned. Sitting in his death-row prison cell, Watts distinctly remembered the rooster's bloody slaughter. A defining moment in his life, the exact moment in time when he had learned about cause and effect, how there are karmic consequences for one's bad actions.

Decades later, the state of Vermont, with its newly reinstated death penalty, was about to reinforce the notion that there are karmic consequences for one's bad actions.

His last supper arriving at his cell door interrupted his nostalgic reverie. Death row guards solemnly delivered the condemned prisoner's special meal preceding execution:

A massive, 96-ounce beefsteak spilled over the edges of his dinner plate, dripping blood, prepared just the way he had come to prefer: Bloody raw. The meal was proffered with the compliments of the house. "Bon appétit," said the little placard on the tray, signed by Governor Mort Grimes himself. The governor had even gone to the trouble of drawing a smiley face below his signature.

There would be no T-Shirt with this Ole 96er.

Sigh.

And because Watts was on suicide watch, neither would he be provided with a fork, knife, or a spoon. No napkin would be provided. Might hang himself. With a napkin?

John Michael Watts hungrily tore into his last meal with bare hands and teeth, licking every last drop of blood and grease from his fingers. He licked the plate. A rivulet of blood trickled down his chin. The succulent feast of raw meat reminded him of his time with his old friend Blind Charlie at the crash site.

As a tribute to his grandmother, Madge Watts, he washed down the bites of raw steak with a quart mason jar filled to the brim with lime green Kool-Aid, poured from a pitcher with slices of oranges floating in it. Just like grandma used to make for him all those summers ago. He toasted her in absentia.

Michael John Watts had disobeyed humankind's social contract, and for his mortal sin, he was about to be severely punished. "Don't piss off, grandma," he muttered to himself between bites.

Chapter Fifteen

Ordered by the authority of the superior court of the state of Vermont, the death sentence was to be carried out at 6 am on the 12th of October. Method of execution: Electrocution.

A bright sunny Monday morning, the skies were robin's egg blue. Not a cloud was to be seen from horizon to horizon. Visibility was unlimited. An excellent day for flying mused Detective Donner.

Both Detective Donner and Prosecuting Attorney Klaus Dickner had traveled to witness the execution in the state's name. All totaled 32 witnesses gathered in the observation room that resembled a mini Rialto movie theater. Replete with four rows of eight seats each, each tier rose from just enough higher from the proceeding row so everyone would be assured of a clear view of the proceeding. Donner and Dickner took their assigned seats in the front row. Donner rocked back in his seat. Unlike a movie theater, these seats did not recline.

A black curtain hung in front of the room, where the silver screen would have been if it had been the Rialto. Someone drew back the curtain, revealing a glass observation window lending a clear view into the execution chamber. All in attendance watched as a pair of correctional officers led Michael John Watts shuffling into view escorted by the chaplain.

Warden Smears entered the observation room, took the podium, and announced to the witnesses, "Good news. There are no stays. Be over soon."

Michael John Watts took his seat in the electric chair.

Guards removed his handcuffs, then strapped his chest, arms and legs securely to the shiny wooden chair. His shaved skull glistened, ointment having been applied to optimize the conduction of the electricity.

Michael John Watts vacant eyes searched the crowd behind the viewing window for familiar faces. He nodded to one of the 32 witnesses, an elderly woman, a grandmotherly type, wearing a cheap blue print dress with a floral pattern and shod in worn work boots. Tears streaming down her face, she returned a forced smile.

Warden Smears asked Michael John Watts if he had any last words.

He hesitated for a moment. Finally, voice quavering, he said, "I give my love to my family and friends. Farewell. In particular, grandma Krempaski who taught me the proper way to shuck red rippers."

Jim Coleman, his lawyer, nodded solemnly in acknowledgment. So too did Fred Gump, the prison chaplain who had spent the night with Watts in prayer.

Watching through the glass panel, Donner, Dickner, grandma Madge Krempaski, and the other observers heard Michael John Watts mumble his last words, something droll about how Rock and Roll would surely save the world. And how much he was going to miss red rippers.

The stern-faced guard slipped a black hood over the condemned man's head, effectively covering his features, rendering Watts an anonymous caricature, a no-name entity. All the while, the chaplain continued to intone biblical wisdom about the valley of the shadows, forgiveness, and meeting one's maker.

Dickner nudged Donner and whispered, "What's a red ripper?"

Donner raised his shoulders. "Dunno."

Pointing at Watts through the window, Donner said, "With that hood on, he looks like that gimp character in the basement of the Pulp Fiction movie. Know who I mean?"

The elderly woman dressed in a simple blue cotton dress and shod in work boots turned to stare at him incredulously and said in a thick accent, "Sir. Have you no respect?"

"Respect," Donner said, jerking his thumb in the direction of the electric chair, "That guy's an animal."

She pointed a stern finger at him. "I know who you are," she said. "You're the detective who put my boy in that killing chair. Mark my words. One day you'll get yours. Get what's coming to you full and well. You'll see."

Dickner nudged him gently in the ribs and whispered, "That's the infamous Madge. Remember her from the trial? Always crying and carrying on. Judge Smith had to tell her to shut up or leave the courtroom."

Donner furrowed his eyebrow and shook his head to show he had no recollection whatsoever of who she was.

Dickner went on to explain, "You know. It's Grandma Madge Krempaski. The chicken lady." He made a chopping motion with his hands to mimic chopping off a rooster's head with a hatchet then mimicked, "Bawk, bawk, a bawk," giving a fair impression of a hungry chicken scratching around a hen yard."

"Oh," he nodded. He got the connection.

"Sorry, ma'am," he turned to her, "Gallows humour, meant to lighten the moment. No disrespect intended."

Grandma Madge's jaw gaped wide open. Her face turned crimson red, fully from ear to ear. She began to weep softly. "No disrespect intended? I curse you. I curse you to damnation!" She began to cry softly.

With the onset of weeping, Donner remembered her courtroom drama and. How after a succession of outbursts, Judge Smith ordered the bailiff to escort her out of the courtroom and how she had bitten the deputy in the arm, drawing blood.

Dickner nudged him in the ribs again and murmured, "Gallows? I can't believe you just said that to her. Did you say gallows to a woman whose grandson stands poised before the proverbial gallows? Got any guillotine jokes?"

Someone turned off the lights in the viewing room, highlighting what was going on inside the brightly lit execution chamber.

It was time.

Inside the death chamber, guards pulled a thick strap across Watt's mouth and chin to immobilize his gimp-garbed head so it wouldn't violently jerk to the side when they applied lethal voltage.

The guard

 turned to the warden.

Warden Smears nodded, giving the go-ahead.

The gallery of observers poised to watch the condemned man draw his last breath.

Unseen in a back room, an anonymous executioner pushed the button. Two thousand volts surged through the wires making an audible 60-cycle hum.

Watts's body tensed.

His hands tightened into clenched fists.

He moaned, writhed.

He made choking sounds, jerking around like an epileptic suffering a terrible seizure.

Wisps of white smoke arose from his gimp hood.

Even though Watts was in another room, Donner could smell the rank odor of cooked flesh, the effect more than a little reminiscent of the pungent odor he remembered from the Blind Charlie crash scene years before.

A minute later, the machine was turned off.

The humming stopped.

Watts went limp.

Dickner murmured, "He was an evil man. Needed

killing."

Donner nodded, "Yessiree. Without a doubt. Sumbitch deserved to die if anybody did."

The lights in the viewing gallery came up slowly, from dim to full brightness. For a spell, the witnesses sat in dead silence, their eyes gradually readjusting, all the while continuing to stare at Watts slumped lifelessly in the electric chair.

In time, a white lab-coated doctor sauntered in, unbuttoned Watt's blue prison shirt, placed a stethoscope on his chest, and listened for a heartbeat. Looking at the warden, he shook his head, no. The doctor aimed a light into Watt's be-stilled eyes. The pupils did not dilate. At 6:10 am, Michael Alan Watts was pronounced one dead sumbitch.

Grandma Madge sat in a chair sobbing and sniffling into her handkerchief.

Donner stood, stretched, and casually took steps towards Madge.

Dickner smiled, thinking Detective Donner would offer a word of condolence to bereaved grandmother Krempaski. Poor woman.

But that nicety was not to be.

With an exaggerated flourish, Donner mimicked sniffing the air as if he were trying to identify a peculiar smell in the room.

Madge stopped weeping long enough to scowl.

Having gotten her attention with his parody sniffing, Donner began to hold his nose and said in a voice just loud enough for her and no one else to hear, "Your grandson smells like burned French fries, don't you think?"

Like a shot, Madge stuck her finger smack dab in Donner's face and growled, "I'm warning you. Don't piss off, grandma."

Chapter Sixteen

During the morning rush, radio station WBZ Boston's breaking coverage reported Watts died in the electric chair at 6 am that morning after a night of weeping and praying and gorging on a beefsteak.

A Shiretown Standard newspaper article run the day after the execution would quote Madge Krempaski as saying," He'll always be my precious grandson. Regardless of what he did, he was still a human being. And I loved him so much it hurts."

Jim Coleman, Watts' attorney, spoke of his client's passing simply saying," He entered the execution chamber silent. He left silent. This is where it ends."

John and Ginny Coleman, death penalty abolitionists and witnesses to the execution, argued capital punishment amounted to torture, unnecessary cruelty, tantamount to disembowelment in public, being stoned to death, being burned alive, or beheaded. "It's positively medieval," the couple posited.

Fred Gump, the prison chaplain, revealed how Watt's last hours on earth had been spent weeping and praying that the condemned man had expressed great regret for what he had done on the side of the mountain.

The article also quoted the detective who had investigated the case and bore witness to the execution. Detective Kurt Donner was quoted as saying, "I felt no compassion for Watts whatsoever. He had an easier death than his victim. Wish I could have been the one flipping the switch."

The Shiretown Standard article wrapped up its coverage on the execution by explaining how Watt's last meal on earth had been a 96-ounce beefsteak, six pounds of meat, gristle, and fat, how Watts had wanted it that way as a tribute to Hollywood actor John Candy and his Movie, in the movie the Great North Woods.

In an article appearing months later, Rolling Stone would point out how Watts added insult to injury by plagiarizing late, fellow band member Alan Lage's catchphrase, "Rock and Roll would save the world." So it seemed disgraced Watts had not only been a murderer but also a shameless, word thief.

Chapter Seventeen

At about the same time the lights flickered upstate on death row, a construction crew was poised to start work at Edgar Hill's old farmstead. A flock of crows perched in pine trees overlooking the spectacle unfolding before them. Now many years after the incident, and despite the fresh weather on this particular October morning, the ruins of the barn still stank of the dead.

In the intervening years after the trial and succession of appeals, the property had come to be known as Lone Grave Bluff. Townspeople still spoke in whispered tones about the macabre tale of Blind Charlie's murder and cannibalism. Some storytellers claim during cold winter nights, in heavy snow, you can faintly hear faint riffs of Rock and roll music emanating from the ruins of the burned-out barn. The most commonly heard song was Led Zeppelin's Stairway to Heaven.

But on this day, there was only the sound of a flock of crows caw, caw, cawing in the treetops at least until the construction equipment fired up its diesel engines and drowned them out.

Property taxes were unpaid because Edgar had fled and was no longer around to pay any of his bills. The government seized the farmstead property and went on the auction block. A real estate conglomerate out of Boston bought it at a tax sale for pennies on the dollar. The corporate minds were intent on paving a parking lot and building condos made of ticky-tacky, all looking just the same. Suffice it to say. The new owners were eager to get to completion and a Return On Investment.

To that end, a big orange, Pemberton Construction Incorporated (PCI) backhoe busied itself shoveling ashes and bits of charred wood out of the barn's floor and depositing the debris in a dump truck to be hauled down to barges in New Jersey for disposal at sea. The work proceeded uneventfully for a couple of hours.

Until there was a shrill, screeching sound as the bucket hit something metal, sending a flurry of orange sparks in the air.

Work halted immediately.

Hendry Smith, the operator, slid down off his seat and shuffled forward to see what was wrong.

"Well, shut the front door," Hendry said, kicking at what appeared to be nothing more imposing than a piece of flat, rusty sheet metal exposed in the dirt. The crows were going nuts, caw-cawing like there was no tomorrow.

"What is it?" asked Binnie Smith, walking up. He was worried they had uncovered a bundle of bones from an indigenous gravesite or some such thing. This situation would shut down the operation until lawyers sorted it out. That would mean billable hours, and lawyers would make piles of money sorting it out while he sat on his hands in limbo.

PCI would bleed dollars.

Hendry stood staring at the metal debris. Hooking his thumbs in his suspenders, he shrugged his shoulders," Dunno. Something metal. I guess. Still got paint on it."

"Looks like the roof of a car," added Binnie, lifting his sunglasses and squinting. "Whatever it is, been in the ground a long time."

"You know how cousins Edgar and Wilbur were when they farmed this land. Could be anything at all."

Over the years, the brothers Smith had uncovered some strange things at construction sites, never buried riches, lost holy relics, or a corpse. Nothing seriously strange, just weird stuff like broken wheelbarrows, vintage motorcycles, and a surprising number of old leather shoes.

Binnie twirled his finger in the air, making the classic hand gesture for, Let's roll! "Keep digging. We're burning daylight. Time is money." He clapped his hands together, "Let's get going."

Hendry sighed, then climbed back into the cab of the Case backhoe loader and resumed methodically pulling bucketfuls of earth out of the ground in front of, in back of, and to the sides of the metal debris.

Patiently, Binnie stood by, watching the slow progress.

As the hole in the ground grew broader and deeper, the dank odor of cow piss began to permeate the Autumn air, a common occurrence with disturbed, former pastureland and cow barns. With the hole now dug two feet deep, they could see an intact windshield and a hood ahead of a roofline.

"What the heck?" said Hendry, his voice trailing off.

When Binnie saw a Rolls Royce hood ornament poking up out of the pile of dirt, it piqued his curiosity. "Interesting," he said, walking closer to the edge of the excavation to get a better look.

On his brother's direction, Hendry swiveled his machine a few degrees to the one side and began digging anew behind the cab. In a dozen bucketfuls, he had unearthed enough dirt to expose the remnants of what looked like a homemade pickup's cargo bed consisting of rotten dimensional lumber and side stakes.

Hendry kept excavating. Dumping one of the buckets of dirt onto the ground, buried treasure magically appeared, scattered in the dirt like diamonds. More particularly, what had once been a case of Narragansett beer spilled out onto the ground.

Binnie plucked one of the green glass bottles off the

ground and shook it. Empty. Bone dry. No church-key had ever popped its top. Long ago, rust had perforated the caps. Over the years, the brew had spilled out into the ground. "What a waste of perfectly good beer," he muttered, shaking his head in disgust.

"And our favorite brand," shouted Hendry, over the roar of the backhoe's diesel engine.

The next find: A cache of quart cans of motor oil, the old-fashioned kind of container where one had to poke a hole in the top to pour the lubricant into the engine's valve cover. Those, too, were rotten from so many years buried in the soil.

Binnie made a hand gesture across his throat, the classic signal to halt digging.

The engine slowed to an idle. Once again, Hendry climbed down out of the cab. The two brothers stood by the side of the hole, staring intently at whatever it was they had unearthed.

The brothers looked at each other and said simultaneously, "Agnes."

In a quiet voice, Binnie said, "Wondered where the old girl has been for all these years."

While Hendry went back to digging, Binnie called the Shiretown Police Department to report his macabre find.

They told him to shut down the dig.

Binnie Smith defied the order, telling the dispatcher to go stuff himself. After all, Edgar and Wilbur were family, first cousins on their mother's side.

Little by little, the excavation continued, revealing first that it was definitely a vehicle, and secondly, that yes, it was Edgar Hill's beloved pickup truck, Agnes.

Finally, Hendry's digging revealed its last haunting secret: Three decomposed bodies sitting next to each other in the front seat. Three skulls grinned maniacally.

Binnie recognized Wilbur and Edgar from their wild,

unkempt, gray beards and shaggy, shoulder-length hair even in decomposed death. Effie Mae was doubtlessly seated between her brothers, recognizable from her long shaggy, bleach blonde hair.

Within an hour officers, Thorndike and Barnhardt had shown up in their police cruiser and were busily stringing rolls of yellow crime scene barricade tape around the perimeter.

The coroner was on the scene soon after that. "Likes his work a little too much," some folks in town whispered about him around the cracker barrel at the Buggy Whip.

Before Binnie and Hendry had fully unearthed the passenger cab, the coroner predicted that they would find nothing more than bones garbed in rotten clothing. The lack of any putrid smell meant there would be no stinking, rotting flesh. Just bones. So naturally, it followed. No one in attendance bothered to suit up in Tyvek coveralls or booties.

Immediately after dispatching officers Thorndike and Barnhardt, Shiretown's Police captain had phoned Donner, who was still upstate with Dickner at the prison.

Donner said he would be at the crime scene as soon as possible. A couple of hours drive down from the state prison. ETA late afternoon at the latest.

Curiously, Detective Donner never showed.

Not ever.

Searching the property for clues, Thorndike and Barnhardt police found a weathered backhoe on the back of the property, hidden in a machine shed under a rotting tarp. Was it used to bury the victims, the cops wondered?

But the real eyebrow-raiser came when Thorndike checked the steering wheel and control levers for fingerprints. Someone had carelessly left a full set on the wheel. Somehow the impressions had survived intact through several winters.

All the cops would have to do was run the prints, and
hope for a match, to determine the identity of the mass
murderer. Easy ID.

Chapter Eighteen

It was said of Doctor Timothy Drevyanko that he enjoyed his occupation as a forensic pathologist a little too much. Do not misunderstand. He was hardly a ghoul. Which is to say it wasn't that he enjoyed dissecting cadavers, but instead that it was in the interpretation and analysis of what he found post mortem that offered him satisfaction. And it was undeniable that he was very good at what he did.

Within a couple of days of uncovering rust-ruined Agnes and her three deceased passengers, coroner Drevyanko's forensic examination concluded someone all three victims in the head, at close range. Bullet fragments were recovered from the bodies. In his analysis of the physical evidence, Drevyanko determined that Edgar, Wilbur, and Effie Mae had each died from a single gunshot to the head, with all three bullets fired from the same .38 Special revolver. From the striations, the rifling marks engraved on the spent bullets, they appeared to have been fired from a Colt snub-nosed revolver, probably a Detective's Special.

Drevyanko further concluded that about the time of the murders, someone had excavated a hole inside the barn, arranged the corpses in Agnes' front seat. Rolled the pickup into the hole, then entombed the Rolls Royce with the victims seated inside buried under four feet of dirt, cow manure and straw.

Important to note was his conclusion that the murder and burial would have occurred years before the ill-fated De Havilland Beaver had crashed into the barn setting it ablaze.

Further, during the autopsy, the coroner also determined that post mortem, someone had mutilated all three corpses. A crude incision in their abdomen had allowed the perpetrator to raise the flap of abdominal skin and expose the internal organs. Each victim's liver was missing a slice, a crude resection.

Had the killer taken a slice of liver meat as a trophy, Drevyanko wondered? Was this a ritual killing? What other reasonable explanation could there be for the mutilation? Macabre, mused coroner, Drevyanko, eagerly anticipating sharing his findings with Detective Donner.

"Evidence," Detective Donner would have declared, index finger dramatically pointed in the air. But Donner was nowhere to be seen.

The motive for the mutilation did not matter to Drevyanko. However, the details and particulars of the Hill triple murder would make the case a tantalizing prospect for his next article in the American Journal of Forensic Medicine. He would have to get busy writing it.

Chapter Nineteen

orth Carolina State Trooper, Hub Alligood, liked spending time on the road because the road was always full of surprises. Hub had pulled over an older man for exceeding the speed limit in his late-model Cadillac. Hub wondered if this particular traffic stop would prove uneventful or surprising. Or not pan out. For him, historically, every one of life's events was like the Lady or the Tiger. You never knew.

"Speed limit's 55 miles per hour 'round these here parts," he politely told the violator.

"Didn't think I was going that fast."

"Laser snitched you out, Mister Jenks. Says you were doing 75 miles per hour. Twenty over the limit. A moving violation."

In denial, old man Jenks shook his head, "Driven hundreds of thousands of miles, never had an accident. First time I've been pulled over." Jenks, thin gray-haired and wearing gold-framed glasses, looked like a Baptist preacher. In truth, he sold life insurance policies to tobacco and pig farmers by the bucketful.

"Ever wonder how many accidents you may have caused over the years unknowingly?" said Hub.

"I'm just a poor county boy out there with the chickens and the pigs. No, sir, no one has ever pulled me over. Not so much as a warning ticket, not in all my life."

Hub had already conducted an FBI wants and warrants check, which verified John David Jenk's claim of no record was true. "Well, this is your lucky day, Mister Jenks. I'm a-gonna give you a friendly little warning. Reminder to hold it back just a little."

Hub handed Jenks a clipboard with the ticket clipped to it, telling him, "Signing is not an admission of guilt, just an agreement you received this warning. Sign at the bottom. You get the pink copy."

"I appreciate that." Old man Jenks signed, then handed the clipboard back out the window.

In return, trooper Alligood handed him back his license and registration.

Jenks smiled, "Well, you're a nice young feller. About as old as my youngest son."

"Won't happen again, will it, sir."

Jenks paused for a moment before replying, "Nope. You got my word."

Hub nodded. "Okay. Have a nice day."

Hub got back in his cruiser and waited for the older man to pull out. Then a minute later, he took off. His thoughts were already somewhere else, on food, more specifically the food served at Black Betty's Wagon Wheel Cafe.

Growing up in rural North Carolina, Hub's family had been dirt poor. Parents divorced, there was no dad in what they called a broken home back then. Some mornings he and his two little brothers would find baskets of donated food on their doorstep. In the summertime, for weeks on end, their only food was a monotony of grits for breakfast and boiled sweetcorn on the cob for supper. No butter.

Typically, his school lunch, packed in a brown paper bag, was a single sandwich wrapped in waxed paper, made with thick slices of momma's homemade bread, generously buttered with lard. There was no meat, no government cheese, not even peanut butter, let alone grape jelly.

Sometimes, like a pack of starving wolves, he and his two brothers would pick up and devour orange peels the other kids had cavalierly discarded in the lunchroom trash bin. So it should come as no surprise to learn that Hub had significant food issues as an adult, sometimes eating two lunches and two dinners on the same day.

In his early days as a state trooper, one of his captains had taken him aside to advise him, "Never let them issue you a pair of britches bigger than size 38s."

Hub managed to control his weight for a couple of years. At best. Suffice it to say, ten years into his career, he had blossomed some and was bigger around the middle than he ought to be.

Most mornings, at first light, Hub lay in bed in a half-awake, half-dream state, thinking about his coming day, fantasizing about what he would eat and where he would eat it. While some men ate to live, Hub lived to eat.

Earlier that morning, before coming on shift, Hub had eaten his first breakfast at the Cottage Inn. He had wolfed down a Lumberjack Breakfast:
- Four eggs over easy
- A rasher of bacon
- Three sausage links
- A thick slice of country ham
- A big mess of crispy hash browns with onions and green pepper topped with grated American cheese

The Cottage Inn's Lumberjack portion was so generous it was served on two platters: Taters and eggs and meat on the other. Suffice it to say, Hub was the kind of man who ate the filling out of the middle of a peach pie but never quite got around to the crust, even those lovingly baked with lard.

Now the middle of the morning, he decided to stop off at Black Betty's for an early lunch. He had a powerful hankering for Betty's pulled-pork sandwich: A half-pound of smoked wild boar, served Carolina Style on a homemade potato roll along with a side of creamy, yellow coleslaw.

Conveniently, Betty's was just down the road a mite, outside of Elbow Lick township, a few minutes away. Hub would exceed the speed limit by 20 miles an hour to get there a couple of minutes sooner. A moving violation even for a cop.

During the drive, he thought about his life experiences being a cop, how he had pulled dead, mangled bodies from wrecked cars. How he had held the bloodied hand of a dying mother, looked into her eyes and lied, reassuring her that her dead child would be okay, then watched the life fade out from the young mother's eyes.

He'd been attacked by women while arresting their husbands for severely beating them the fourth or fifth time. The term domestic abuse did not do justice to the vile act.

Hub had performed CPR on a dead man because doing so made the family members feel better that he had at least tried. He had chased fugitives from justice through the piney woods of the Uwharrie National Forest, been in high-speed car chases, been in car crashes, been hospitalized, been in a coma.

Hub had once been about to squeeze the trigger, about to kill a man, when the perpetrator finally came to his senses, dropped his handgun, and put up his hands in surrender.

Yes, the road was always full of surprises.

What would today bring, he wondered? The Lady or the Tiger?

Chapter Twenty

It was a mystery, thought some.

As the days followed the discovery of Miss Agnes, it was as if Donner had disappeared from the face of the earth. Just as Edgar, Wilbur, and Effie Mae had disappeared decades before.

A week after the Smith brothers/twins uncovered the grave of their cousins, Edgar, Wilbur, and Effie Mae, the only other living creatures at the crime scene up north in Vermont was a flock of crows, poking their beaks in Hendry's piles of dirt. Donner would neither visit the crime scene as a perpetrator nor as a detective in charge of the case. This was for the simple reason he had fled the jurisdiction.

In a couple of days driving, Donner had escaped as far south as the coastal plains of North Carolina. Hungry and needing a pit stop, he decided to take a break on the outskirts of Elbow Lick, at Black Betty's Wagon Wheel.

Off the beaten path, the place was a good ten miles off the interstate, a circumstance that guaranteed cheaper gasoline and lower-priced food.

A roadside diner, Black Betty's Wagon Wheel, décor was themed country inn, offering Southern cooking like good old mom used to make. Only it wasn't mom slaving away over a hot stove. It was Black Betty, the proprietress. Or, perhaps, Donner grimaced, some guy nicknamed Stinky held hostage in the back so he wouldn't bother folks none.

Donner arrived mid-morning, after the breakfast rush and before the lunch trade. So naturally it followed, the parking lot was pert-near empty. There were only three cars. One was a white Chrysler 300, another vehicle a nondescript, gray Audi sedan, and the third, a subcompact Kia sporting a custom yellow and black paint job, lending it a strong resemblance to a bumblebee. Appropriately, the vanity license plate declared:

BUMBLEB

Donner wondered whether the plates and custom paint job were a tribute to the pollen-gathering insect or the robot superhero character and buddy of Optimus Prime and Galvatron.

The inside walls of Black Betty's were painted contractor's white. Appropriate to its country inn theme, it was garishly decorated with pitchforks, steel tractor seats, and rust-speckled bushel baskets fitted with hemp rope handles. Alongside the cash register proudly stood a restored antique corn shucker, done up in tractor red, wet-look red, a color no self-respecting farmer would allow within a country mile of his corn crib.

Prominently displayed on the wall hung a print of a homespun-garbed farmer and wife, with the farmer gripping a three-tined pitchfork. This was no faithful reproduction of the famous oil painting, American Gothic. Instead, it was a down-home parody. The faces of man and wife were of Black Betty and Burt Reynolds, a photo-shopped image the made it appear Burt and Betty were taking a selfie, Burt's arm extended holding an iPhone.

One foot in the door, Donner noticed how the place was squeaky clean. Black Betty herself was busily mopping the floor. "Welcome, welcome. Sit wherever you like," she offered. Looking up from being down on her hands and knees, she rendered a big smile. "Bee will take care of ya'."

Donner figured she was called Black Betty for the reason she was a raven-haired beauty, or, at least likely, had been in her youth. Nonetheless, her head of hair was beautifully jet black and lustrous. At her age, probably dyed, he figured.

A customer was just leaving, standing at the counter getting change.

"Want some iced ice tea to go?" the waitress asked.

The man put his wallet in his back pants pocket. "That sure would be nice, Bee. Thanks."

"Getting hot as blazes out there," she added. "Come noontime, and you'll be glad you did."

Bee plucked a Mason jar glass off the counter where the man had been sitting, transferring the dregs of it into a tall paper cup. She sloshed it around a mite. "Needs a tad more ice," she said, generously topping it off with ice and a healthy slug of iced tea. "This should hold ya 'all 'til lunch," she smiled.

The man nodded his thanks, took a sip of iced tea, and left without another word.

Donner took a table near the front door, right upfront. The waitress arrived table side within mere seconds. Matronly, but pretty, long, brown hair streaked with gray. Bee's earrings were a bundle of fuzzy, black, and yellow yarn, twisted and turned to resemble a bumblebee. Donner thought if they hadn't been so big, the bugs could have been fishing flies. He tagged Bee as the likely owner of the yellow and black Kia parked in the lot. BUMBLEB as in Bumble Bee, as in Bee, he mused. It didn't take a genius to figure that out.

In a hurry to get back on the road, Donner didn't bother picking up the menu Bee had laid down on the table. He wasn't interested to learn if grilled venison slathered with Amish horseradish, roast of wild boar dragged in from the swamp by Jim Bob, or sauteed kangaroo lips imported from Australia, or Ethiopian deep-fried hippopotamus ear were the specials. Only to be told, "Sorry, sold out." of anything exotic on the menu that might have tempted him.

He ordered iced tea.

"Sweet or unsweetened?"

"Sweet, of course. And burger and fries."

"Carolina style?" Bee southern drawled.

"What's Carolina style?" he asked.

"Burger smothered in meaty chili topped with a generous dollop of crispy slaw."

"What kind of chili?"

"Lean ground beef, brown sugar, apple cider vinegar, mustard, chili powder." She narrowed her gaze. "You're not from around these parts, are ya'?"

Donner sighed. "No. Why?" he said defensively. "You about to tell me you're fresh out of burgers Carolina style?"

"Course not, honey. Just wonderin'. Y'all talk funny," she drawled.

"Chili, not too spicy, is it?"

She shook her head, no.

"Alright, I'll have the Carolina burger."

"Single or double?" she asked, up-selling.

"Double."

She left Donner to sip his Mason jar of sweetened iced tea, tea so ice-cold it gave him brain freeze.

Waiting for his order to come up, Donner considered his precarious situation. From his long career as a Law Enforcement Officer, he knew there would be a thorough investigation, and in time he would be linked to the triple murders of Wilbur, Edgar, and Effie Mae. He didn't know what mistake he had made at the crime scene. Didn't matter. Perps always do. Why should he expect his fate to be any different, he reasoned.

Being a former cop sentenced to prison, his long-term chances for survival would be slim to none. As a former cop with more than one enemy in the joint, he would be marked for death. Some inmate who needed cigarettes, or sex, would accept a contract to stick a shiv in his belly and twist it around in his guts or knock him down a flight of stairs. Perhaps a gang of thugs would corner him in the shower room and beat him to death for the hell of it. With the death penalty recently reinstated for the crime of murder, he also had that delightful possibility to look forward to.

He began to chuckle. On the bright side of things, it would almost be worth it to watch the bumbling ass, Dickner, try to prosecute him.

The waitress broke his reverie, putting the Carolina burger and fries platter in front of him.

It smelled good.

"Here ya go, sweetie," Bee drawled. "They eat sloppy, so I brung all y'all extra napkins."

"Thanks." Donner thought she seemed nervous.

Both arms folded across her chest, her voice tense, Bee said, "I'm fixin' ta go out back and help Betty with something important. Ya' all sit tight. Back in a minute."

A moment later, Donner heard a screen door slam shut. Hungrily, Donner took a bite of burger. Bee was right. It was messy. And delicious.

Preoccupied, he ate, all the while cursing himself for having craved Edgar's exotic guns so badly he had made the trio disappear. Most violently. Then stealing their weapons from the evidence locker with a fake auction. A search warrant followed by a look-see inside his own gun safe would reveal that fact, and that would give investigators motive.

Edgar, Wilbur, and Effie Mae were reaching up from a common grave condemning him. In unison, the three dimwits pointed bony fingers at him down in North Carolina. He could almost hear their ghostly voices crying out in unison, "Guilty!"

Donner sighed.

Punishment loomed.

Just not right away.

Eventually, he would be caught. A traffic stop for speeding or having a burned-out taillight. Something petty. There would be a trial. A conviction by a jury of his peers.

A string of appeals would line the lawyers' pockets but make no difference in the inevitable outcome.

An appeal would only delay his inevitable fate.

One day in his future, there would be a prisoner's special meal preceding execution. His last meal on earth, Donner mused morbidly.

He would make it raw liver. Venison liver, if possible, he decided. And then, with the rising of the morning sun, would come punishment.

Donner thought back to the day of Michael John Watt's execution, his remark about the gimp mask, his lame gallows humour excuse, Watts' grandma, and the ominous curse she had laid upon him.

In his peripheral vision, outside in the gravel parking lot, he spotted a commotion. He looked to see what was going on. Five North Carolina State Police cruisers had wheeled into the lot, kicking up gravel. They parked, not grouped closely together like cops do when meeting for lunch, but instead fanned out in a wide array across the broad expanse of the parking lot in a tactical formation.

At that moment, Donner came to the realization he was alone in the Wagon Wheel. The inside of the restaurant was stone, cold silent. "Hello," he called out. His voice echoing off the walls was weird, he thought. Black Betty was visibly absent, along with her mop and bucket. So too was Bee, the waitress who had told him, "Sit tight. Back in a minute."

Yeah, right. With the cops.

Spotting a folded newspaper lying on the counter by the register, he got up and walked over to retrieve it.

Outside in the parking lot, he could

see Black Betty and Bee standing behind one of the patrol cars, huddled up with a gaggle of troopers engaged in deep conversation.

All the troopers cradled shotguns in the crook of their arms. Probably 12 gauge Remington 870s fitted with riot barrels and loaded with six rounds of double-odd buck. Did any of the troopers have an itchy trigger finger, he wondered.

Bee was pointing towards the restaurant, jabbering away. Still holding her mop, Black Betty nodded excitedly. The troopers were listening intently.

Donner picked up the newspaper from the counter. Right there on the front page, above the fold, his washed-out driver's license photo stared back at him in brilliant colour. Big, black headlines under his picture proclaimed:

Mass Murder Suspect Flees

The caption below his photo warned how fugitive from justice, Kurt Donner, was presumed armed and dangerous. The story proper told the tale of the alleged triple murder of Edgar and his siblings and how Donner was on the run. A nationwide manhunt for the cop-gone-bad was underway. Have you seen this man, it asked? A most generous reward was offered for his capture.

Donner chuckled, figuring Black Betty and/or Bee had recognized him from his picture in the morning newspaper and dropped a dime on him. So it looked like he wouldn't be snared in a traffic stop, after all.

Reinforcements arrived. Three more state troopers kicked up gravel pulling into the lot, immediately followed by four more Morton County deputy sheriffs, all of them in one big hurry to deploy their firearms and perhaps be on the nightly news.

Donner accepted his plight: Trapped inside Black Betty's Wagon Wheel and outgunned.

Chapter Twenty-One

Outside in the parking lot, there was nary a hint of a breeze, just the red hot sun getting ever hotter as the day went on. Other than the caw-caw-cawing of the flock of crows perched high up in the pine trees, it was deathly silent. The troopers, having finally donned the bulletproof vests they were already supposed to be wearing, were beginning to wilt. In sharp contrast to their pressed, sharply-creased trousers, wet patches of sweat spread in great circles under their armpits. They began to stink of body odor.

The temperature was pleasantly cool inside the restaurant, with the air conditioning set to a comfortable 74 degrees Fahrenheit. A thermostat setting is cool enough to keep guests happy during their meals, yet not so comfortable they linger after finishing dinner. Donner calmly marked time, comfortably sipping iced tea and reading the paper.

The trooper assigned to megaphone duty fired it up. "Kurt Donner, we know you're in there." He demanded Donner come out with his hands up, generously giving him all of five short minutes to make up his mind.

Or, what? Be shot? Surrender? Not very damn likely, mused Donner, abandoning his meal on the table and immediately seeking cover and concealment behind the counter. Might have a sniper, he mused.

After about a minute, the trooper repeated his demand, that Donner give himself up, advising he now only had four minutes. A trooper's practiced stern voice, combined with the countdown, were intended to strike fear into the heart of a fugitive.

Unfazed. Donner did nothing.

He was a cop. He knew the game.

A full five minutes came and went.

A phone started ringing somewhere inside the Wagon Wheel, startling him. Donner spotted it on the wall behind the cash register. That would be the trained negotiator calling, the guy who would try to talk him into surrendering into their custody.

Donner let it ring. He knew the troopers in the parking lot didn't really expect him to come out with his hands up.

If he did, great.

If not, it didn't matter.

Donner knew the troopers on station were assigned to secure the perimeter, preventing his escape, effectively killing time.

Eventually, a SWAT team would arrive in its specially-equipped van. Heart racing and healthy doses of adrenaline and testosterone flowing in their veins, the team members would dutifully suit up in bulletproof vests then lock and load their well-oiled Colt M4 assault rifles. When they were good and ready, they'd shoot a volley of teargas grenades through the big front window and storm the restaurant like Omaha Beach. Depending on the department budget, they might even throw in a stun grenade or two to make things fun.

It would be a textbook operation. For years afterward, the police academy would show cadets video highlights of the operation and brag about how it had been brilliantly executed. "Here's how it's done, boys."

The academy would likely neglect to mention Black Betty's tort claim for the significant damage done to her restaurant: The fire started by the tear gas grenades and the substantial loss of revenue during reconstruction.

So it goes.

Drawing his concealed-carry Colt Detective's Special snub-nosed revolver from inside the waistband holster, Donner wheeled the cylinder making sure all five chambers were loaded. He wondered how Crow Killer Johnson would have handled such a predicament. Come out shooting, or stand fast and defend the fort? He was dead certain there was no way Johnson would have surrendered.

Peering around the end of the counter, he watched a dark blue SWAT van amble into the lot and squealed to a halt behind the array of what had grown to be a combined total of 15 state police and Morton County patrol cars.

"Time's up," crackled the voice in the megaphone.

The notion that he might have to shoot and kill a fellow Law Enforcement Officer in a few short minutes to get out of his predicament bothered Donner greatly. He had always thought of himself as one of the good guys. Now, this?

Get out of his predicament? He scoffed at the notion. Not likely, not alive.

Donner gripped the Colt in his right hand, lovingly caressing the two-inch barrel with the fingers of his left hand. It was an ugly gun, its blued finish stained with rust.

The pistol, a trophy from his gun collection, belonged to Linda Allay, the beautiful blonde, Linda, his first suicide case. Her splattered blood and brains had severely corroded the blued finish while it had sat uncleaned in the evidence locker awaiting trial.

Holding Linda's former handgun, a chill ran up and down his spine. The revolver felt oily and evil. Donner truly believed evil emanated from its steel frame as if the revolver was possessed by a malevolent demon, one who had tormented Linda into killing herself.

The Colt had that eerie effect on him from the first moment he had pried it from Linda's cold dead hand, her fingers sticky-wet with dried blood. At first touch, it had felt oily and malevolent like an evil spirit possessed the gun.

Sometimes, late at night, reposing cozily in his den, fondling the revolver, he had wondered what perverse illogic the gun's demon had whispered to Linda convincing her to end her own life, convincing her to make a permanent solution to her temporary problem.

Sitting on the floor behind the counter at Black Betty's, with his back against the wall, Donner talked to the Colt like it was a dear old friend. In a smooth, reassuring voice, he asked, "My sweet, sweet 38. You have always been there for me. With Edgar, Wilbur, Effie Mae, and all the others. Tell me. How do you want to handle this one?"

Donner bowed his head and began to weep.

She spoke.

Chapter Twenty-Two

Hub sat in his cruiser outside Black Betty's with the rest of the troopers and deputies, killing time listening to old school Country and Western tunes on the radio. Patiently, Hub waited despite his growing need to pee and his stomach grumbling in protest. Hub was as hungry as a starving wolf. But with the Sheriff's SWAT team poised to deploy, there was nothing to do but impatiently wait. And wait some more.

Until a single gunshot rang out from inside Black Betty's diner.

The unmistakable sound got Hub's attention. The big flock of crows perched in the pine trees, also patiently waiting, began caw-cawing, but curiously, they did not alight from the trees and fly off. It was as if they wanted to see what happened next in the ongoing human drama.

Hub switched off the AM radio and got out of his cruiser.

Dumbfounded by the gunshot they had heard from inside the restaurant, the SWAT team members looked at each other in wonderment.

"Weren't we supposed to fire tear gas grenades through the window and storm the place?" asked a young one.

"We going inside or not?" asked someone else.

"Maybe we ought to do like we planned," said another.

"The gunshot. Figure he topped his-self?" said somebody.

Confusion reigned in the ranks.

Hub, having had enough, sighed, shook his head, and began walking towards the place's front door. "Goin' ta get me a Coke-cola, Betty," he told the owner. "I'll be sure to leave money on the counter like I always do."

The others watched in awe as Hub went inside Black Betty's, leaving them standing in the parking lot looking like fools.

As Hub came alongside the suspect vehicle, a Fire Cracker Red Jeep Wrangler, as having been detailed in the APB, Hub deliberately slapped the driver's side taillight. Marking the red lens with one's fingerprints was a smart cop trick intended to leave evidence, to document that you were there with that particular vehicle. Because out on the road. You never know what surprises are going to happen.

Hub drew his Glock 19 pistol. Inside he found Kurt Donner behind the cash register, lying in a pool of his blood on Betty's formerly clean-scrubbed floor, gripping a snub-nose revolver in bloody fingers.

He was quite dead.

Hub was sure the man was dead because most of the top of his head was missing. Blood, gray matter, and a flap of scalp decorated the wall.

"Like a dropped Halloween pumpkin," Hub murmured, holstering his Glock.

A few moments later, the SWAT team, followed by a gaggle of troopers and deputies, had worked up enough nerve to follow him inside the place. Black Betty and Bee were a few steps behind.

Like a herd of cows grazing in a pasture, the cops tromped around the crime scene, compromising the integrity of the evidence, pointing and laughing, making gallows humour about the poor Yankee detective lying dead on the floor.

"I get the gun," said Captain Jim Crowe. "I want it. It's mine. Somebody put it in an evidence bag, label it and give it to me for custody."

Hub stuck his hand inside an evidence bag, turned it inside out, knelt, pried the Colt from Donner's sticky fingers, and zip-locked the baggie closed. This was not his first murder investigation. His method allowed picking up evidence without smearing blood on the outside of the bag.

"Has it been fired?" asked one of the younger cops, in a failed attempt to appear knowledgeable.

"Yeah, I'd say it's been fired," came Crowe's sarcastic answer, pointing to the dead body and the abundance of red and gray brain matter splattered on the wall.

"Guess there won't be a perp walk for the media," someone said.

From the first moment Hub touched the Colt, a shiver ran up and down his spine. Through the thin walls of the plastic evidence bag, the Colt felt oily and malevolent, as if some demon's evil spirit emanated from its steel frame. To Hub. It felt like his soul had descended into a depressing, dark space.

Anxious to be rid of it, Hub immediately laid the evidence bag with the Colt inside in the waiting hands of Captain Crowe. Instantly the malevolent feeling left Hub.

Crowe held the bloodied Colt up to the light, admiring it inside the baggie. "My sweet, sweet little .38," he smiled. "After the attorneys and courts are done with her, she's going into my private collection. You can count on that."

Hub's stomach growled loudly.

One of the deputies joked," That you Hub, or maybe the Yankee's wantin' a bite of Miss Betty's fine home cooking."

Hub wondered if he could convince Bee into making a pulled pork sandwich for him, served Carolina style. "Say, uh, Bee, any chance I could get a pulled pork sandwich? I am powerful starved."

By then, some of the deputies were taking selfies with dead Donner. One of them got down on the floor beside Donner and had one of his buddies drape Donner's arm over his shoulder and take pictures. Apparently, it was worth it to him to ruin a perfectly good uniform shirt to get the selfie.

One of the troopers reached down to get a fingerful of blood and then playfully flicked a droplet at one of his buddies.

Someone in the crowd passed gas, a loud fart that sounded and reeked like it was from a water buffalo.

All of them giggled like schoolboys.

"That didn't sound like Hub," said one. "Not loud enough or smelly enough."

"Well, it sure wasn't the perp passed gas." said another.

"Corpses do that," said the young one in an attempt to appear knowledgeable.

"You boys," said Black Betty, shaking her head, laughing aloud with them. A dead customer lying on the floor behind the register didn't seem to bother her one iota. Burt Reynolds starred down from his portrait with an animated grin. He, too, was enjoying the show.

"Flip the Yankee over onto his belly," growled Captain Crowe.

They did.

Without saying a word, Crowe reached inside the evidence bag, took out the Colt, and carefully aimed at Donner's cadaver.

"What ya' going to do, chief?" asked one, chuckling, "Shoot him."

Crowe did not answer.

In time, he deliberately squeezed the trigger, rapid-firing four times: Bang, bang, bang, and bang. All four lead slugs grouped in a tight pattern on Donner's right buttock. Each time one of the slugs dug into the flesh, Donner's dead body twitched like it had been kicked in the ass. With the fifth squeeze of the trigger, the hammer fell on an empty chamber, and the pistol went, click, instead of bang.

The gun went click for the simple reason that particular model Colt, a concealed carry model, only held five rounds in its cylinder. Donner had fired one shot, followed by Crowe's four shots. One plus four equals five. And Crowe had never learned to count his shots, not even when excited.

No big surprise, the Colt's booming reports, fired in the confined space inside the restaurant, had been tremendously loud. Hub's ears were ringing. So too were everyone else's. Some of the men worked their jaws, trying to make the ringing go away.

"Nice shooting, Tex," Hub said sarcastically. "Think you got him?" The two men did not get along. Years before, Crowe was one of the guys who harassed Hub about never letting the Highway Patrol issue him with britches larger than a 38 waist.

Crowe scowled at Hub, took a step forward to kick Donner hard in the ass. "Damn Yankee," he muttered. Grabbing a paper napkin out of a counter dispenser, he wiped the smear of blood off the toe of his shoe then discarded the blood-soiled napkin on the floor.

Crowe pointed at dead Donner, saying in an angry voice," This here's the sumbitch what got Madge Krempaski's grandson executed. What goes around comes around."

Crowe pulled out his smartphone and took a picture of Donner, showing his face and the top of his exploded head, then messaged it to Grandma Krempaski, who just happened to be his mother's aunt.

"Kharma's a bitch," muttered someone.

Crowe took a deep breath, held it, then exhaled. Calmer, he rationalized aloud, "Sumbitch made a break for it. Fleeing felon. All y'all are witnesses. Am I right?"

Dumbfounded at what Crowe had just done to the corpse, evidence, and the crime scene, the troopers and deputies all nodded in agreement, not wanting a confrontation with their superior.

That is, except for Hub, who in his own mind had already moved on to a critical matter: Finally getting something to eat.

"That the guy all y'all are after?" asked Bee. Standing at dead Donner's feet, being careful to avoid stepping in the puddle of blood, she pointed to a burger and fries platter on one of the tables. "That was his meal." Shaking her head in disbelief, she added, "Fool didn't know what a Carolina Burger was. Had to explain to him like a child."

"Yankee." scoffed someone.

Crowe's face turned ashen. Pointing at Donner's former table, he quietly said, "That table right there, Bee. That the one where he was sitting?"

Bee nodded. "Yep. Man barely touched his food."

"We are in deep trouble," said Crowe, shaking his head in disbelief. "Ain't no way this guy was a cop. Look at where the table is. Right upfront. In front of God and country. No cop with half a brain would'a done that. Even rookie cop know to sit in the back, out of the way, to keep an eye on things."

"Looks like y'all shot the wrong man," said someone in a worried voice.

"Appears to be so," added another, unconsciously stepping back as if to distance himself from what had transpired.

"Well," said Hub, shrugging. "He was a Yankee cop. Maybe he didn't know no better."

"Wait a minute," said Crowe, pointing his finger in the

air in a Eureka moment. "Let's not panic yet. Somebody check his back pant's pocket for a badge and ID."

"You mean, check him where you shot him?" said someone sarcastically.

"Least you didn't shoot him in the back," said another.

"Backside's bad enough," said the young one shaking his head in critical judgment.

"Maybe you should reload and shoot him again. Keep shooting until he's for sure dead.," said Hub.

"When you're checking him for ID, look

 for ammo too. That's a .38 Special was in his hand. All I have is 40 S&W for my Glock, or I'd lend you some rounds," said another.

Crowe glared at his compadres.

The Colt, warm to the touch from rapid firing, felt heavy in his hand, like a ten-pound dumbbell at the gym. His trigger finger itched. "Yeah, dig around for some more ammo in his pockets, why don't ya'. Probably got a speed loader or loose rounds. I want to reload. Just in case."

Hub, standing by Donner's former table nibbling on stone-cold French fries, got Bee's attention. "Say, uh, Bee, dear. If you're not too busy, I'd take that sandwich now, if you please."

"Carolina style, did you say?"

"Yes, ma'am. Yes, I surely did."

"Coming right up." Bee critically looked Hub dead-in-the-eyes, then at Donner's french fries, and back again in Hub's eyes. "Fries too?"

"Yes, please. Dead man's fries are cold." He dropped the fry he had just taken a bite out of, back into the waxed, deli paper-lined red basket. "And a dab of yellow slaw," he smiled. "If you don't mind, none."

Hub removed his broad-brimmed, state trooper's hat, placed it on Donner's former table, pulled out the chair, and sat. At least the seat wasn't still warm from Donner's behind, he mused.

Once again nibbling on dead man fries, Hub was already thinking about supper, wondering where later on he might find a slice of sweet, pecan pie for dessert, topped with a generous scoop or two of vanilla ice cream.

Yes, sir, the road was full of sweet surprises.

Something in Hub's peripheral vision caught his attention. He paused his daydream of sweet pecan pie long enough to turn and see Crowe in a far corner where any cop with half a brain would sit so he could keep an eye on things. Sitting Yoga-style on the floor, he was busy admiring fondling the snub-nose Colt revolver, whispering to it. Crowe went silent for a moment, staring at it as if listening intently to some mystery it was privately revealing to him and him alone.

Crowe occupied himself with staring at the revolver in his hands right up until the moment when one by one, he loaded five brass cartridges in the cylinder's chambers and swung the crane closed. He closed his eyes. He took a deep breath and held it.

All eyes on Crowe, the restaurant was deathly silent. When the cooler's compressor motor cycled on, it began humming in a 60-cycle, monotone vibration. Startled by the sound, Hub jumped.

Someone caught Hub's eye, circling his index finger next to his temple, the universal gesture for crazy, implying Crowe was so far out crazy not even the Greyhound Bus Line could bring him back to sanity.

A cold shiver reverberated up and down Hub's spine. On instinct, he immediately got up out of his chair and headed for the door.

Bee, carrying Hub's pulled pork sandwich and fries platter, along with a heaping side of yellow coleslaw on a second plate, walked into the dining room. Watching Hub walk out the door in such a big hurry confused her a mite. "Hub?" she called out after him. "Hey. Come back! Got your sandwich..."

Hub did not answer.

He was already out the door and halfway to his cruiser.

"Well, shut the front door," said Bee in exasperation, shaking her head in disbelief. She had never seen Hub walk away from a meal before. Especially one on the house.

Hub did not stop.

Hub's momma may have been a dirt, poor, country girl, who couldn't keep a man, but she sure didn't raise no fool, he mused. All the way to his cruiser, Hub wondered if he would hear the gunshot before making it out of the parking lot.

The End